C000300018

Literary Cats

LITERARY CATS

Judith Robinson & Scott Pack

BODLEIAN
LIBRARY
PUBLISHING

In memory of my wonderful mother, who introduced me to the world of books and who always believed in the writer in me. JR

In memory of all the cats who have deigned to share my house with me, especially Uma, the only one that actually seemed to like me. And for Alfie, the current incumbent. SP

First published in 2022 by the Bodleian Library
Broad Street, Oxford OX1 3BG
www.bodleianshop.co.uk

ISBN 978 1 85124 573 4

Text © Judith Robinson and Scott Pack 2022
Illustrations © Wendy Wigley, 2022

Publisher: Samuel Fanous
Managing Editor: Deborah Susman
Editor: Janet Phillips
Picture Editor: Leanda Shrimpton
Production Editor: Susie Foster
Cover design by Dot Little at the Bodleian Library
Designed and typeset by Lucy Morton of illuminati in 11½ on 16 Fournier
Printed and bound in China by C&C Offset Printing Co., Ltd.
on 120 gsm Chinese Baijin Pure woodfree paper

British Library Catalogue in Publishing Data
A CIP record of this publication is available from the British Library

CONTENTS

INTRODUCTION

CATS FEATURE AS CHARACTERS IN THE VERY FIRST books that are read to us as children, right through to the timeless literary classics which readers everywhere have known and loved. They accompany some of the most famous human characters in writing of any genre, be it literary fiction, science fiction or poetry. When we look back to the earliest examples of storytelling – the myths and legends that form the foundation of our literary culture today – cats make a regular appearance and are portrayed as rich and entertaining characters. If we pay close attention, we can discover paw prints in the most unexpected of places. Our mission in writing this book has been to make visible the indelible imprint that cats have left on the literary world throughout the centuries.

ANCIENT ORIGINS

Across the globe, cats have established themselves firmly in our human world, sharing our homes as beloved pets. But before we delve further into the pages of a multitude of cat stories, we should ask ourselves: where did the shared journey of humans and cats begin, and how did the cat come to be such an integral part of our imagination?

Felines and humans share a turbulent history, their relationship ever-changing. Cats have been both worshipped and persecuted, adored and detested in equal measure. Today, we may recognize them as intriguing animals and adorable pets, but at various stages in the past humans have viewed cats as magical beings, as incarnations of goddesses or the Devil himself. What remains today of these beliefs are stories, myths and legends which still influence our contemporary attitude towards our feline companions.

The origin of the domesticated cat lies on the African continent, more precisely in Egypt. In their usual elegant and discreet fashion, the wild ancestors of the domesticated cat surreptitiously sought out Egyptian villages to hunt mice and other rodents, as well as snakes.[1] People realized how useful and pleasant these animals were and so the wild cats were slowly domesticated and adopted as members of the family.[2] As early as 1950 BCE cats started to appear in Egyptian depictions of everyday life.[3] It is here that the cat first emerges as a pet, cherished and enjoyed by all members of the family. By

1450 BCE the cat was a popular, if not *the* most popular, domesticated animal in Egypt. Images of cats started to appear on tomb walls and reliefs, as participants in domestic life. Often, these artistic depictions showed cats sitting under chairs, especially a woman's chair.[4] This is evidence of the long association between women and cats, a relationship which took a darker turn in medieval times, as we explore later.

As Egyptians became more familiar with their newly domesticated feline companions, they noticed the animals' extraordinary physical abilities, which far exceed those of humans and can, at times, seem almost supernatural. Their senses are highly developed; cats were believed to be able to predict the weather, earthquakes and even death. Egyptian society therefore assigned the cat a mystical and spiritual depth which ultimately elevated them from their domestic status to something much more complex and intriguing. Egyptians believed that all of nature was suffused with a divine spirit and interpreted the cat's extraordinary abilities as manifestation of this spirit. This transformation can be seen as the origin of the cat as a literary character – when humans began to weave stories, myths and legends around this creature that shared their homes. The animal began to transcend its existence as a mere pet, evolving into a being of higher order and even an incarnation of certain deities.[5]

The most prominent of those feline deities was Bastet, or Bast, who was regarded as a protector of women, children and the home, forming a strong association with fertility, childbirth and motherhood. Every year, the city of Bubastis hosted a magnificent five-day festival celebrating Bastet. The Greek historian Herodotus gives an account of witnessing these celebrations and claims that 700,000 people attended, which indicates how cherished the goddess was.[6]

As domesticated cats thrived in Egypt, it was unavoidable that this popular animal would travel beyond Egypt's borders. International trade, especially via ships, allowed the animal to spread to the European continent, initially via Greece, and further afield, spreading through Persia and India to the Far East. In Greece cats made frequent appearances in arts and literature from around 500 BCE onwards. The beliefs and characteristics associated with the animal travelled with them, to some extent, and were absorbed into local cultures. Herodotus himself, in his account of the celebrations in Bubastis, points to this amalgamation of beliefs, as he refers to Bastet as the Greek goddess Artemis. Artemis, daughter of Zeus and twin to Apollo, was also connected to fertility and childbirth, as well as the hunt, and was known to turn herself into a cat at times. Artemis later became associated with Hecate, goddess of the night and the underworld. Ovid's *Metamorphoses* tell the story of Galinthias, servant to Alcmene, who brought the wrath of Hera, Zeus' wife, onto herself. Alcmene was due to give birth to Zeus' son Hercules, but Hera was doing her utmost to prevent the birth. Galinthias intervened and tricked Hera's helpers, allowing for Hercules to be born. In her anger, Hera transformed Galinthias into a cat (or a weasel in some versions of the story) and Hecate eventually took pity on her and adopted her as a priestess, further emphasizing the cat's connection with the underworld. The worship of these goddesses also translated into Roman society, finding its equivalent in Diana, who reflected many of the attributes of Bast and Artemis, and other associated deities.[7]

The attributes and associations which were assigned to the cat in ancient times, through religious beliefs and mythology, seem to have had an influence on the cat in folklore in Europe and beyond. As we will see, many of the feline characteristics described above continued to fascinate humans, so much so that their fascination found expression in popular folk tales and fables.

FABLED ANIMALS

Some of the most famous examples of early literary felines are included in Aesop's fables, which make a rich contribution to the treasure trove of cat stories. It is not known for certain where these fables originated or how many individuals contributed to them. Aesop may or may not have existed – he is rumoured to have lived in the sixth century BCE, whereas the first collection of fables was recorded in the tenth century CE.[8] Nonetheless, the fables as they exist today are still widely read and many have been absorbed into popular culture.

In 'The Fox and the Cat', the cat's relaxed cleverness is celebrated. The fox brags about the many tricks he can use to escape his enemies. As they hear a pack of hounds, the cat speedily jumps up the tree whilst the fox debates which trick to use for such a long time that he ends up being caught by the dogs.[9]

In 'The Cat Maiden' we can recognize the cat's connection to ancient deities as Jupiter and Venus debate whether it is possible for creatures to change their very nature. Jupiter is convinced that it is possible; Venus disagrees. To prove her wrong, Jupiter transforms a cat into a young maiden. The maiden marries a human and appears to have in fact fully adapted to her new appearance and status, playing the young bride beautifully at the wedding feast. Venus, meanwhile, is not convinced and releases a mouse in front of the bride – who duly forgets about her new role as blushing maiden and pounces on the mouse. The female goddess has proved her point: we cannot deny our very nature.[10]

Some fables do not let the cat claim the victory, such as 'The Cat and the Mice'. When a cat discovers a house infested with mice, it promptly decides to make its home there and sets about decimating the mouse population. The mice decide to remain in the safety of their homes, hoping that their enemy will eventually tire of waiting and leave. The cat decides to utilize its acting skills and plays dead, hanging upside down from a peg on the wall. But on this occasion the mice do not fall for the cat's clever trick, as they know how devious these animals can be.[11] Despite being written millennia ago, *Aesop's Fables* contain cats with traits and personalities that will be just as recognizable to modern audiences as those of Ancient Greece.

A cat also makes an appearance in *Reynard the Fox*, a beast fable which was recorded as early as the twelfth century and the origin of which is difficult to pinpoint, with scholars assigning its early incarnations to Flanders, Germany and France. The eponymous fox has upset most of the animals gathered at the court of the lion Noble, king of all animals. Led by Isengrim the wolf, many animals complain to the king about Reynard's devious behaviour, whereas Tibert the cat initially rises to his defence. He is later chosen as the king's messenger to speak to Reynard, on account of being 'wise and wary'. But even feline intelligence cannot protect Tibert from the clever fox's tricks on this occasion and he falls prey to a trap set by Reynard. In contrast to some of Aesop's fables, the great feline intelligence is not harnessed to trick other animals, but to deliver fair judgement. Unfortunately, his opponent is the ultimate trickster of the animal world.[12]

At this point, it is important to look beyond European folklore; as global trade routes continued to grow, the cat reached cultures across the world and found its way into stories, myths and legends further afield.

In India the *Panchatantra*, a collection of ancient Hindu tales, includes the story of the supposedly devout and wise cat who is approached by a hare and a partridge to help them settle an argument. As the two animals approach the cat, he pretends to be old and deaf, asking them to come closer, all the while winning their confidence by reciting prayers. As they approach, convinced by his apparent wisdom, he strikes and kills them both. A version of this story is also often included in collections of Aesop's fables, which suggests that cat stories travelled just as much as cats themselves did.[13]

In Buddhism the cat was viewed with some suspicion, as a cat allegedly prevented Buddha from receiving life-saving medicine by killing a mouse on a mission to deliver the tonic to him. Despite this story, Buddhist monks in Thailand valued cats as rodent hunters, helping them to preserve ancient scrolls.[14] In Bengal a witch called Chordewa appeared in the shape of a black cat.[15]

In comparison, the prophet Muhammad took a much more positive view of cats – it is said that he was extraordinarily fond of his cat, and that markings on the cat's head were left there when he stroked it. He was once saved from a snake by his cat; the tale goes that he rewarded the animal for this selfless deed by giving it the ability to always land on its feet.[16] His affection for his cat was so great that he carried it in his sleeve; not wanting to disturb it, one day he went so far as to cut off his sleeve to allow the animal to rest. Muslim societies in medieval times valued the cat as a vermin hunter, particularly in cities, and the Muslim faith still considers cats exceptionally clean, approving of their lengthy grooming rituals.[17]

A cat appears in one of the stories in *One Thousand and One Nights*, the collection of folk tales originally told in Arabic. The cat in question comes to the aid of Ali al-Zaybaq, a thief and swindler, who is known as Mercury Ali because of his quicksilver-like ability to escape capture. On arriving in Baghdad, Ali's belongings are stolen by serial con-artist Dalilah the Crafty; Ali needs to break into her home to get them back. He does this by 'accidentally' bumping into her cook in the marketplace, getting him drunk and taking on his persona. However, once he is working in Dalilah's house, suspicions are aroused; Ali, still pretending to be the cook, has to prepare a meal for the household with the watchful eyes of Dalilah upon him – but, being an imposter, he doesn't know his way round the kitchen. This is where the cat comes in, for the actual chef has a pet cat who usually plays companion to the cook, and by following this cat Ali manages to find his way through the garden to the larder, gather the food and return to make dinner. He drugs the meal, searches the house while its inhabitants are unconscious, locates his belongings and returns to his original mission. The cat, despite the help it gives Ali, receives not even a stroke in thanks.

It is likely that the cat reached Japan around the seventh century, travelling via Korea and China. Cats were cherished as rare pets by the Japanese aristocracy; they also helped to safeguard silkworm cocoons from rats.[18] Japanese culture also assigned cats magical attributes, of both a threatening and a helpful nature. Along with other animals, such as the fox or badger, they appear in several stories in Japanese folklore.

In one such folk tale, a boy sets out to hunt with bow and arrow. His mother urges him to take one additional arrow. The boy is not successful in his hunt and, as night falls, he takes a break from his endeavours, gazing at the moon. Soon, a second moon appears in the sky and the boy suspects it to be of a demonic nature. He shoots his remaining arrows and hits the target with the final one. The mysterious object emits a scream and falls to earth. The boy finds in its place a large dead cat. When he returns home and tells his mother about his adventure, she admits that she saw a cat the previous day, eyeing up his arrows and counting them. She suspected foul play and hence made her son take another arrow to fool the cat.

One of the most cited and blood-curdling Japanese stories is the tale of the vampire cat. A large cat killed and took the identity of O Toyo, the Prince of Hizen's favourite female companion. Neither the prince nor anyone else noticed the difference, and the cat, under O Toyo's disguise, continues to visit the prince at night, depleting his life force. A loyal retainer manages to watch over the prince, staying awake despite the cat's magical powers by stabbing himself in the thigh with a dagger. He therefore eventually uncovers the mystery that O Toyo is, in truth, a vampire-like cat monster. It transforms itself back into its cat shape and escapes, only to be found and killed later. The prince recovers.[19]

Another legend, set on the island of Sado, provides a much more benevolent view of the cat. An old, poor couple had a black cat which they adored and fed despite their long-lasting poverty. Eventually the cat decided to help the old couple and transformed itself into a geisha. Any money she earned from entertaining her patrons was given to the couple. She entranced customers, in particular with her dancing skills, but the cat did not enjoy her profession very much. When a client discovered her true identity, she made him promise not to tell anyone. He, of course, could not help himself and shared her secret with others. As soon as he had broken his promise, a black cat descended from a large cloud and snatched him up, and he was never seen again.[20]

DEMON CATS

Returning to the European continent, as culture and religious beliefs evolved, so did the reputation and status of the cat. Although pagan beliefs and traditions never completely vanished, Christianity became the dominant religion and exerted a great influence on how people viewed the world and creatures around them. Any worship of animals as representatives of divine beings would have been taboo – the Egyptian belief that all creatures carried within them a divine spirit did not agree with Christian theology, where humans were acknowledged as beings superior to animals. As we have learnt, cats were particularly associated with cults and beliefs centred upon female deities and focused on female concerns, such as childbirth. As women's social status changed due to Christian doctrines, the animal often associated with women's issues was also affected.[21]

In the thirteenth century Pope Gregory IX explicitly connected the black cat to the Devil in his decree *Vox in Rama*. His inquisition claimed to have collected evidence, extracted under torture from people they deemed heretics, that the Devil appeared as a black cat in satanic rituals. Several accounts of witch trials include stories about women changing into cats, having cat familiars or being visited by the Devil in the shape of a cat. Pope Innocent VIII issued a papal bull in 1484 ordering all witches and their cats to be burnt at the stake. The infamous *Malleus Maleficarum*, or

The Hammer of Witches, also claims that witches regularly changed into cats.[22]

The association of witches and black cats is one we are familiar with today – it forms part of our popular culture and is replicated every year as part of Halloween celebrations around the world. Perhaps it is the beauty and mystery of the cat which has contributed to this enduring image – much as we have a continuing fascination with stories about magic and witchcraft, as we will see in some of the following chapters.

PET CATS

In the seventeenth century the Enlightenment eventually brought about a marked change in beliefs and challenged superstitions, which also affected the reputation of the cat. Its tarnished reputation was somewhat reinstated, and it became a popular pet to the aristocracy. This marks the beginning of a new period of literary responses to the cat, some of which we explore in the course of this book.[23]

We may well recognize the images and characteristics which these stories evoke, so embedded have they become in popular culture. Although they have evolved and changed over time, our image of the cat today is still shaped by myths and legends which can be traced back to Ancient Egypt.

Popular culture reflects the complex nature of our relationship with the cat – an animal which is seen both as a cuddly pet and as a fiercely independent creature. These attributes are precisely what makes cats so fascinating to us and why we may prefer them to other pets. Cats will happily join you on the sofa, purring and full of affection. Equally, they will set off on their own adventures, day and night, roaming the outdoors, sometimes returning after a hunt with their prey or displaying the scrapes and gashes of a hard-won battle. We may not worship them as incarnations of a goddess anymore, but we can still recognize that elusive spirit which convinced the Ancient Egyptians that cats were Bastet herself.

In the following chapters we explore how the relationship between humans and their feline companions has been recorded and reflected in literature. Each chapter focuses on a particular genre or a particular role which the feline characters fulfil, ranging from cats in poetry to celebrated literary classics, and including talking cats, as well as those feline characters that are simply unforgettable. As we get to know each cat, we explore what makes them so special, what they bring to each story and plot, and what they might mean to the author and the reader.

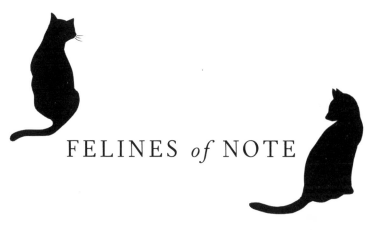

FELINES *of* NOTE

C ATS ARE MERCURIAL CREATURES, DIFFICULT TO
grasp in both the physical and the metaphorical sense:
one minute you find them happily sleeping in their favourite
spot at home, and the next they are gone, most likely prowling
the neighbourhood via their secret passages and shortcuts.
Equally, they change from affectionate pet to fierce predator
in an instant. Nonetheless, there are some feline characters in
literature that have a more lasting presence – perhaps precisely
because they intrigue us so with their multifaceted nature and
stay with us long after the page has been turned.

THE FIRST FAMOUS CAT

Puss in Boots is one of the most popular cat stories and can
rightfully be considered the one which established many
commonly accepted aspects of feline nature in our imagination. The story was first recorded in the sixteenth century,

but Charles Perrault's version from the late seventeenth century is most well known. A miller's son is disappointed when he inherits nothing but a mere cat after his father's death. He is convinced that his inheritance will only provide him with a bit of meat and a small piece of warm fur, when he suggests eating and skinning the cat. But the cat transpires to be much more. On hearing that he is about to become dinner, he instantly makes himself indispensable by means of his prowess as a hunter as well as his general cunning and ability to develop elaborate plots to secure his master's future. This eventually leads to the young miller's son winning the heart and hand of a princess, as well as the ownership of rich lands and a castle. Although this is a tale full of magic, including, of course, a talking cat, the plot mainly relies on feline intelligence. *Puss in Boots* lays the groundwork for many other stories explored in this book – it develops the character of the clever feline, which uses its natural abilities to trick evil adversaries and to overcome any barriers placed in its way.[24] In the chapter 'Talking Cats' we revisit this story when we explore Angela Carter's unique interpretation of the original tale.

FAMOUS FELINE COMPANIONS

We need to flash forward a couple of hundred years to meet the cat that makes an appearance in Truman Capote's

Breakfast at Tiffany's. The feline character is a memorable feature in the famous film adaption of the novel and its function as plot device has been analysed by many. The role earned its feline actor, Orangey, many accolades, including a Patsy, the animal equivalent of the Oscar. In the novel, we first meet Holly Golightly's cat as the unnamed narrator observes both the cat, 'a red tiger-striped tom',[25] and Holly enjoying the sunshine on the fire escape. From here on the cat is a constant presence in Holly's apartment. The narrator, or Fred, as Holly refers to him, observes that Holly is very affectionate with her feline companion, although 'it was a grim cat with a pirate cut-throat's face; one eye was gluey-blind, the other sparkled with dark deeds.'[26] At the same time, Holly refuses to become too attached to her pet. She does not give him a name as this would only be appropriate if he belonged to somebody, and she claims that theirs is a casual relationship, where both parties remain independent. She is not ready to call a place her home, to settle down and attach herself to anything or anyone. Of course, the fact that she carries the cat around whilst hosting a party somewhat belies her claim. Even as she is arrested for her peripheral involvement in a drug cartel, she remembers to ask Fred to feed the cat in her absence. The cat seems a fitting pet for the character of Holly Golightly – the independence that these animals display matches Holly's need for freedom. Like a cat, she roams the night, doing as she pleases.

But when Holly eventually decides to leave the city, Fred is shocked to see her abandon the cat in a strange neighbourhood, roughly shooing him away to seek a new home. Although she tries to defend her actions, she chokes on her words, in emotional turmoil after abandoning her loyal friend. Almost instantly, she changes her mind and frantically tries to find the cat again, but he has disappeared. She finally acknowledges to Fred that she and the cat did belong to each other. Fred promises to find the cat after Holly leaves and he indeed eventually spots him through a window, quite comfortable in a new home. Throughout the story the cat offers silent emotional support to Holly, much as Fred does. She does not want to acknowledge any feelings or relationships which could tie her down, prevent her from finding the elusive perfect life she is chasing. When she admits to the emotional attachment to the unnamed cat, she also implies an attachment to the narrator and the possibility of an alternative love and life.

In Doris Lessing's 'An Old Woman and Her Cat' we meet Hetty Pennefather, who lives alone in her tiny council flat in London. Her husband passed away long ago; her children have conveniently forgotten about her. Among the neighbours she has a reputation of being strange. She is described as 'that gypsy woman',[27] referring to her traveller heritage and reflecting her occupation as a rag trader. At a time when she has lost any connection with friends or acquaintances a kitten enters her life and brings her companionship. Tibby grows into a large and feisty tom, who kills pigeons and brings them back to Hetty to be plucked and cooked. She teases him for being dirty and mean-looking, but there is a deep connection between them as neither conforms to society's standards and both cherish their independence. Unlike Hetty's children, Tibby is not ashamed of her. He is loyal and returns home after each nightly hunt. At the same time, he does not burden Hetty with demands, feeding himself, whilst also helping her to shed the loneliness that bothers her from time to time. Tibby accompanies Hetty as gentrification drives her to eventually seek shelter in an abandoned house. He continues to bring her pigeons and warms her at night. Tibby stays with Hetty until the end: they are both a remnant of different times, trying to stay alive in a city that has no room for them.

Whilst these cat characters have a positive, sometimes even nurturing, influence on their humans, some unforgettable felines in fiction are more uncanny, perhaps even frightening on occasion.

SCAREDY CATS

We explore Edgar Allan Poe's undeniable fondness for cats in our 'Authors and their Cats' chapter, but first we will delve here into one of his creations and most well-known feline stories in horror fiction. Published in 1843, 'The Black Cat' is the harrowing account of a man's descent into alcoholism and violence. The unnamed narrator speaks to us on the day before his execution, seemingly wanting to 'unburden'[28] his conscience by providing a true account of what led to his death sentence. He assures us that he used to be a good-natured and kind person, with a fondness for animals, in particular his cat Pluto, given to him by his beloved wife. Pluto is a 'remarkably large and beautiful animal, entirely black, and sagacious to an astonishing degree'.[29] Although the narrator speaks of him warmly, his description evokes the image of an uncanny beast, reminding us of the images of witches' familiars or of witches transforming into cats. This notion is echoed by the narrator's wife, who 'made frequent allusions to the ancient popular notion, which regarded all black cats as witches in disguise'.[30]

Despite his seemingly harmonious and privileged life, the narrator soon finds himself turning to drink, which changes his behaviour dramatically. Alcohol leads him to become violent and unpredictable, eventually abandoning all sense of right or wrong and turning on his beloved cat. In a shockingly brutal act, he cuts out the cat's eye, leaving him alive but disfigured. Pluto's physical deterioration seems to mirror the narrator's descent into alcoholism and his ensuing changing nature, from good-natured to mean-spirited and outright evil.

Pluto's new terror of his owner provokes more and more loathing, leading the narrator to abandon any moral compass and hang the cat from a tree to extinguish the constant reminder of his evil deed. Immediately afterwards, in a seemingly divine act of justice, his house burns to the ground, leaving the narrator and his wife destitute. To his horror, he finds the image of a large cat and a noose imprinted on the one remaining wall. He attempts to find a rational explanation for this, but the supernatural appears to be at play, punishing him for his dark deeds. The story does not end here, though, as the narrator acquires another cat which he encounters in a gin den. Feeling nostalgic, he is momentarily charmed by the cat's resemblance to Pluto. It follows him home and is adopted by the family. The next morning, sober again, the narrator discovers that the cat is not only missing an eye, as Pluto did, but that he also has another distinguishing feature: a large patch of white fur on his chest, which slowly appears to take the shape of a gallows. The narrator's guilt is haunting him in the shape of this cat, which follows him constantly, leading the man to wake 'hourly from dreams of unutterable fear to find the hot breath of *the thing* upon my face, and its vast weight ... incumbent eternally upon my *heart*'.[31] The burden of his sins is manifesting itself as a large cat, and the reader begins to question at this stage whether the cat is indeed physically following him and pressing upon him, or whether it is a trick of the narrator's imagination.

The climax of the story occurs when the narrator attempts to kill the feline in a fit of anger. His wife prevents it, and instead he buries the axe, with which he tried to attack the cat, in her head. The cat disappears. With extraordinary calm and clarity of mind, the man hides his wife's body in the cellar wall. Now that the cat is gone, he seems to have achieved tranquillity and peace, sleeping soundly and not overly worried about being found out. But, alas, when the police search his house repeatedly, the narrator becomes too bold and knocks on the wall that hides his secret, jesting about the excellent quality of the building work. The knock is followed by 'a howl – a wailing shriek, half of horror and half of triumph, such as might have arisen only out of hell'. The police find the body and, perched on top of the head, the black cat, 'with red extended mouth and solitary eye of fire'.[32]

The narrator utilizes the common stereotype of the cat as a demon, leading people into temptation, to blame the animal for the murder. Poe achieves a brilliant double meaning in this tale. On the one hand, the cats in the story are intertwined with common themes of sin, violence and supernatural occurrences. On the other, the cat is depicted as a much loved and loyal pet, equipped with inherent goodness; this ultimately leads to the feline's role of the avenging demon, which brings a crazed murderer to justice. It is interesting that the narrator's wife holds the two cats in great affection and that, ultimately, the cat takes on a companion role, albeit in the afterlife. The connection between women and cats is reflected in this plot twist, hinting at the ancient, mystical relationship described in our first chapter. The cat's ambiguous role stems from the narrator's attempt to justify his actions, of transferring his guilt to an external force, rather than acknowledging that his own shortcomings led to the destruction of everything he supposedly once held dear.

Lady Jane in Charles Dickens's *Bleak House* is also a menacing presence, a constant feline companion to Krook, the unsightly, gin-swilling rag-and-bottle merchant and landlord to Nemo and Miss Flite. She is often found sitting on Krook's shoulder and observing the world 'with her tiger snarl and her club of a tail'.[33] Various characters accuse the large grey cat of cruel and malicious intentions, implying the animal has an uncanny ability to plan and plot, and that she is not what she seems. Miss Flite is particularly concerned for the birds she keeps in small cages in her otherwise bare room. Although she would like to expose her pets to fresh air, she hesitates to leave the window open for too long as she suspects Lady Jane of lying in wait, ready to pounce and attack her collection of 'larks, linnets and goldfinches'. Miss Flite goes so far as to speculate that Lady Jane 'is no cat, but the wolf of the old saying'. She certainly is no cuddly pet and, to most characters in the novel, she seems wholly unpleasant, But, of course, there is one person who cherishes her – the 'disagreeable' Krook.[34] He admits that he initially planned to kill and skin her, as he also trades in cat pelts, among a great many other things. But something made him change his mind – perhaps he recognized a kindred spirit in Lady Jane, as they seem to be well matched and share some characteristics. Krook displays his pride in the cat's vicious nature, having trained her as you would an attack dog. Their bond seems unbreakable: even after Krook's mysterious death, allegedly a case of spontaneous combustion, Lady Jane remains near the pile of ashes and charred floorboards discovered by Mr Guppy and Tony Jobling. So, yet again, we have a feline character which combines several stereotypes of the cat: that of companion and pet, of fierce and skilful hunter, as well as that of demonic companion to a sinister character, similar to a witch's familiar.

When we first encounter the feline Behemoth in Mikhail Bulgakov's *The Master and Margarita*, we get a sense of the novel's surreal and magical attributes. Here is 'a cat the size of a pig, black as soot and with luxuriant cavalry officers' whiskers', which is nonchalantly 'trotting along on its hind legs'.[35] Nothing could be more fitting than including a black cat in Satan's entourage, when he makes an appearance in Moscow in the guise of Woland. The name of the strange feline, Behemoth, again seems oddly fitting. The word 'behemoth' is used in the book of Job to describe an animal and can roughly be translated from the Hebrew to mean 'strange or monstrous beast'. Behemoth the cat does indeed appear monstrous to the unsuspecting people who encounter him. Together with the rest of Woland's bizarre entourage, he wreaks havoc on the lives of a number of people across Moscow, particularly the literary elite of the city. One of their first unfortunate victims is decapitated, whilst another is incarcerated in a lunatic asylum.

Behemoth's humanoid behaviour, including talking and walking on his hind legs, as well as casual vodka-swigging and eating delicately with a fork, unsettles and makes characters believe they have lost their minds. His animalistic or monstrous nature takes over when he is let loose on the compère Bengalsky, fur standing on end, leaping 'like a panther', '[g]rowling', and ultimately decapitating the shocked man.[36] Luckily for Bengalsky, decapitation on this occasion, through some dark magic, does not result in death. Behemoth continues to use his feline abilities to his advantage, when carrying out Woland's bidding, climbing up walls, jumping, leaping and swinging from chandeliers.

What makes the character of Behemoth so fascinating throughout this whirlwind of a novel is the juxtaposition of the monstrous and shocking with the often entertaining dialogue which Bulgakov assigns to the cat. Whilst they are playing a game of chess, the cat is teased by Woland for having gilded his whiskers and put on a white bow tie to attend the grand ball. Behemoth feigns offence and lapses into a pompous monologue, which Woland sees as a diversion to avoid losing the game. But Behemoth assures his master that his 'remarks are by no means hot air, as you so vulgarly put it, but a series of highly apposite syllogisms which would be appreciated by such connoisseurs as Sextus Empiricus, Martian Capella, even, who knows, Aristotle himself'.[37] His ramblings occasionally exasperate Woland, but Behemoth bravely and confidently continues his long-winded explanations and narratives. When we compare this feline demon to those which were rumoured to accompany witches and the Devil himself (as described in the chapter on 'Historic Cats'), we can certainly see similarities – the black fur, the sheer size, the unnatural and, at times, vicious behaviour. At the same time, Behemoth also appears as a parody of these mythical creatures – far less frightening when he opens his mouth to enter into one of his monologues or feign innocence, and even becoming the butt of jokes of his companions.

In Stephen King's best-selling horror novel *Pet Sematary* the feline character embodies the ambivalent attributes which we routinely assign to cats. At the beginning of the novel, the Creed family, consisting of father Louis and mother Rachel, with their children Eileen ('Ellie') and baby Gage, arrive in Ludlow, Maine, to which they are relocating from their former home in Chicago. They are accompanied by Winston Churchill – 'Church' for short – Eileen's beloved pet cat. Although Eileen dotes on him, her father Louis sees a duplicity in the animal, similar to the conflicting attributes that cats were assigned in early storytelling. He witnesses a cruelness in his daughter's pet as Church 'torture[s] a bird with a broken wing, his green eyes sparkling with curiosity and … cold delight'.[38] This realization comes early in the novel and foreshadows Church's transformation later on, following his burial, and resurrection by some unknown evil force, within the ancient Indian cemetery near the Creeds' new home. The age-old folkloristic connection between cats and dark forces makes Church the perfect first victim of the unnatural act of resurrection, although King has spoken before about having been inspired by the demise of his daughter's cat and her heartbreaking reaction to it.

Beyond Church's superficial role as demon cat, he is also a catalyst for some of the most profound life choices and events that humans have to face. Louis felt incapable of having Church spayed in the past because he worried 'that it would destroy something in Church that he himself valued – that it would put out the go-to-hell look in the cat's green eyes'.[39] Louis is protective of his own freedom and independence, occasionally resenting his young family for being so demanding – and he wished to protect this need for independence in Church as well. When he eventually gives in and takes Church to the vet, albeit with great reluctance, he is saddened by the change in Church after the procedure – perhaps because he recognizes the change that becoming a family man and father has brought upon him.

Following their first visit to the pet sematary (a misspelling of 'cemetery'), Eileen is upset by the prospect that

Church will eventually die. Whilst Louis shows sympathy for her emotions, but ultimately insists on Eileen accepting the facts of life, his wife Rachel is enraged that he discussed the inevitability of death with their daughter. The conversation about Church's potential demise exposes a deep trauma within Rachel, leading back to her sister Zelda's untimely and painful death. It is a topic that husband and wife have never fully explored and discussed openly, a dark cloud that hangs over their relationship.

Church's dual role reveals the hidden depths of King's novel – on the surface, it is a horror story, with plenty of scary moments, and eventually also blood and gore. But if we look beyond these obvious aspects, we recognize that King ultimately explores how frightening everyday life can be. The love we bear for those closest to us makes our lives richer, but also brings with it the danger of loss and pain. Experiencing such loss can lead us to the darkest places where we are haunted by the shadows of those we have lost.

Gummitch is a kitten who also lives with a family: mother and father, whom he has nicknamed Old Horsemeat and Kitty-Come-Here, and their two children, the spiteful Sissy and newborn Baby. Gummitch considers himself a superkitten and claims to have an IQ of 160, despite the fact that he cannot talk, 'but everyone knows that IQ tests based on language ability are very one-sided'.[40] Because he is very clever, Gummitch 'knows' that at some point soon he will transition from a small cat into a human child, and that the two children he shares the house with will travel in the opposite direction from human to kitten. 'Space-Time for Springers', a short story by Fritz Leiber from 1958, starts out as a rather sweet tale of a somewhat clever, if deluded, kitten, but slowly develops into something much darker. Sissy starts to tease and torture her baby sibling and the parents either ignore her actions or excuse them. Things get worse, and one night the kitten sees the girl take a hat pin to the sleeping baby's cheek, cutting thin lines rather like cat claws. In what might be an act of protection, or a desperate need to take on human form, Gummitch exchanges souls with Sissy, and in the months that follow her behaviour and intellectual development comes on in leaps and bounds, while the cat grows into a surly and brooding tom. It is a story that presents us with a truly unforgettable feline character and explores the bond between humans and cats to a macabre degree. And 'macabre' is a word that can describe the story that contains our next notable cat.

Following a family tragedy, the true nature of which is only gradually revealed, the surviving members of the Blackwood family – narrator Mary Katherine (known as Merricat), her older sister Constance and their Uncle Julian – live in semi-isolation in their grand old house. Merricat ventures out twice a week for groceries but is always aware of the prying eyes and snide comments of the townsfolk. Back at home, she practises all manner of amateur witchcraft, mainly to keep people away, using spells, totems and the assistance of her pet cat, Jonas. But her magic fails to prevent the arrival of cousin Charles, who proceeds to ruin their protected existence.

In Shirley Jackson's haunting and claustrophobic novel, *We Have Always Lived in the Castle*, Jonas the cat is the only truly innocent character. He is Merricat's almost-constant companion, offering solace in times of trouble and often reflecting her moods – frolicking in the garden on a happy day, skulking in corners at moments of stress – and as such serves as a bellwether for the story itself. And if the reader is happy to accept Merricat as a witch in training, then it is easy to view Jonas as her familiar. There is one charming scene (in a book for which the word 'charming' is rarely appropriate) where Merricat flees from Constance and Charles and takes refuge in her secret garden hideaway.

> I lay there with Jonas, listening to his stories. All cat stories start with the statement: 'My mother, who was the first cat, told me this,' and I lay with my head close to Jonas and listened.[41]

This is the only point in the book where it is suggested that there is some sort of genuine communication between the two. Although it is more likely to be the girl's imagination, it is nice to think that cats have their own version of 'Once upon a time...' that they only share with humans they feel particularly close to.

FANTASY CATS

The world of fantasy fiction has borne some weird and wonderful cat characters. Although *Alice's Adventures in Wonderland* possibly created its very own literary genre, it features one of the most famous fantastical felines. The Cheshire Cat is explored in much detail in the 'Books for Kittens' chapter, but suffice it to say here that the suave talking feline manages to stand out among the many strange creatures which Alice meets in the course of her adventures and may well have inspired other talking literary cats.

Terry Pratchett fans, and there are millions, would be up in arms if our selection of notable felines failed to include Greebo, even though he is probably the most thoroughly unpleasant cat to feature in our book. Greebo first appears in the sixth Discworld novel, *Wyrd Sisters*, and belongs to Nanny Ogg, a wise, friendly and lovable witch, to whom many characters turn for advice and help. She insists that Greebo is a cute bundle of fluff, but more or less everyone else knows that the opposite is true.

Greebo is a battle-scarred, flea-bitten bully who wants to fight, eat or mate with any creature he comes across. He will battle with anybody, has been the victor against at least two vampires, one of which he also ate, and is the master of his own extensive inbreeding experiment. For Greebo is the only male ancestor of thirty generations of cats in Lancre, the town in which he lives with Nanny Ogg. He has mated with and/or fathered every single cat around.

In *Witches Abroad*, the twelfth book in the series, Greebo is temporarily transformed into a beautiful, brainless human who dresses like a pirate and oozes sex appeal. The transformation is not a total success, though, and some of his cat traits remain – he can't work out how to use doorknobs and uses his own saliva to clean himself. From this book on, Greebo occasionally flips between feline and human form.

Despite being what we could generously call a bit of a rogue, Greebo is not entirely fearless. He is scared of a black cockerel named Legba, the Nac Mac Feegle (mischievous fairy-like creatures) and, most daunting of all, a small white kitten called You, who shows nothing but affection towards Greebo, which completely freaks out the old scallywag.

Pratchett appears to have been fond of, and impressed by, cats, as they pop up regularly in his work. *The Unadulterated Cat*, a humorous tribute he wrote to 'real cats', as opposed to the sweet, well-behaved ones we see in television commercials, became an international bestseller, translated into a dozen or more languages. *The Amazing Maurice and his Educated Rodents* is a Discworld novel aimed at younger readers and stars the titular Maurice, a talking cat. He works with a band of rats and a young boy piper, going from village to village as part of an elaborate con. The rats run all over the place, sparking fears of a plague, the piper trots up to lead them all away, and they split the reward money between them. There is also a Greebo-like cat named Guilty in Pratchett's Johnny Maxwell series for children. And Pratchett is often cited, quite possibly erroneously, as the source of a marvellous quotation which harks back to our opening chapter: 'In ancient times cats were worshipped as gods; they have not forgotten this.'

Another significant cat from the worlds of fantasy fiction is Fritti Tailchaser, the young ginger tom who is the hero of Tad Williams's debut novel *Tailchaser's Song*. The book is a classic quest story in which Tailchaser leaves his feral clan in search of a missing friend, Hushpad, after a series of unexplained cat disappearances. On his journey he acquires, and occasionally loses, a number of companions, gets captured, takes part in battles and, of course, learns something about himself in doing so. When he does finally locate Hushpad, he finds that she has become domesticated and lives with a human. Although he stays with her a while, he realizes that he is a feral cat at heart and sets out for home, and presumably more adventures ahead of him. However, more than thirty-five years later, a sequel has yet to appear, much to the frustration of the novel's many fans.

The book owes more than a small debt to *The Lord of the Rings*, something Williams acknowledges with a number of obvious knowing references, and it contains the same well-thought-out internal mythology, complete with gods and ancient stories, songs and traditions. But what particularly appeals is the way Williams anthropomorphizes the cats, and the attitudes and beliefs with which he imbues them. These cats live in a world alongside humans and other animals, but consider themselves as higher beings, more intelligent and superior to those around them, an opinion the cats in our living rooms might share if they had the power of speech.

Before writing the book, Williams considered himself more of a dog person than a cat person, but his wife had cats and, when they moved in together, he grew to like them. He and his wife started creating little backstories and mythologies for their pets, and when Tad reached a point where he was fed up with the various menial jobs he was doing he decided to turn these tales into a novel. It became an international bestseller and was the beginning of a long and successful career.

There are, of course, many other notable cats in literature, far too many to include here, but we hope you have appreciated the small selection we have featured in this chapter. Each of these characters offers a new perspective on fictional cats, adding layer upon layer to the rich tradition of feline storytelling. Our emotions towards these cats may range from fear to devotion, but they certainly provoke a reaction which makes them unforgettable.

CLASSIC CATS

WHILST EXPLORING SOME OF THE MOST ENDURING and celebrated literary works, books that are considered 'classics' today, we are able to glimpse feline characters, albeit only briefly and fleetingly in some cases. It is fair to say that cats in classic works of literature play one of two roles: either they are used as mere metaphors, in the way of describing certain human behaviours in line with our stereotypical perception of the feline character and actions, or they appear as actual characters, playing their part in the plots we know so well.

METAPHORICAL CATS

The stereotypical characteristics and attributes we commonly associate with felines appear to have provided fertile ground for writers, who frequently refer to the animals in painting vivid images of certain characters.

Charles Dickens was fond of cats and they accompanied him throughout his writing life. It follows that cats also regularly appear in his stories. We have already met Lady Jane, the vicious and intimidating feline in *Bleak House*. In his collection of semi-autobiographical journalistic sketches, *The Uncommercial Traveller*, Dickens ruminates on 'shy' or poor neighbourhoods and their inhabitants, including the many animals that live among the human population. He vividly depicts the cat population as barbaric and 'selfishly ferocious'. He describes them as dirty and having lost all pride in their appearance, particularly when they are pregnant. While he briefly mentions tomcats, and how men resemble them at times in their 'exasperated moodiness', women and female cats are dealt with far more harshly – he characterizes both as neglectful of their offspring, argumentative and violent.[42]

The cats of shy neighbourhoods also make a brief appearance in *Great Expectations*, when Pip first arrives in London and is shown to his lodgings by Mr Wemmick, the clerk. Pip's initial impression of London as a grimy, dirty and overall unpleasant place is reinforced by the first glimpse of his new home, Barnard's Inn, where he will share rooms with young Mr Pocket. A jumble of buildings, surrounding a small square which Pip compares to a cemetery and which houses 'the most dismal sparrows, and the most dismal cats, and the most dismal houses'.[43]

Dickens's characters repeatedly use the cat as metaphor to demean women. In *Nicholas Nickleby*, the mad old man who lives next door is in love with Mrs Nickleby but suddenly transfers his affections to Miss La Creevy. Simultaneously, he turns his mad rage to Mrs Nickleby and proceeds to call her 'Cat! … Puss, Kit, Tit, Grimalkin, Tabby, Brindle!'[44] He attempts to shoo her away, like the dirty and dismal cats that Dickens describes in *The Uncommercial Traveller*. The terms 'puss' and 'minx' are also used to describe Miss Squeers's feelings towards Mrs Browdie.[45] Female ambivalence, the combination of affection and deceit, is reflected in *David Copperfield* when Mr Peggotty calls Little Em'ly '[a] little puss', followed by David ruminating on her dual nature 'of being both sly and shy at once', which intrigues him greatly.[46]

Thomas Hardy also compares women and cats, drawing on the sensuous nature of the animal, harking back to its ancient connection with fertility. In *Tess of the D'Urbervilles*, Angel happens upon Tess, who has just woken up. As he holds her tightly, he can feel that she is 'warm as a sunned cat'. A description of her mesmerizing eyes follows, creating a sense of intimacy and sexual tension:

At first she would not look straight up at him, but her eyes soon lifted, and his plumbed the deepness of the ever-varying pupils, with their radiating fibrils of blue, and black, and gray, and violet, while she regarded him as Eve at her second waking might have regarded Adam.[47]

The potentially demonic nature of the cat, as well as sexual connotations, are emphasized in Bram Stoker's *Dracula*, when Dr Seward first encounters the undead Lucy during her nocturnal hunt. He is repulsed by the change in her appearance, remarking on her 'purity [turned] to voluptuous wantonness'. When Lucy sees the party of men observing her, Seward describes the noise she makes as 'an angry snarl, such as a cat gives when taken unawares', with her 'eyes unclean and full of hell-fire'.[48] The description seems to hark back to supposed witches accused of engaging in sexual acts with the Devil in animal shapes, including cats.

In Virginia Woolf's writing, there are several feline appearances, often connecting women and cats. In *Between the Acts*, the cook Mrs Sands dotes on the cat Sung-Yen, saving a slice of fish for him. The narrator later tells us that Mrs Sands does not care much for other animals, but that 'any cat, a starved cat with a patch of mange on its rump opened the flood gates of her childless heart'.[49] It reminds us of the common trope of the crazy cat lady and appears a cruel comment. In Woolf's essay *A Room of One's Own* she also mentions a cat – namely a Manx cat, a breed of tailless cat which originates on the Isle of Man. She observes that it is 'quaint rather than beautiful',[50] something to be pitied and perhaps laughed at. It has been suggested that the cat in this context represents the position of women in a male-dominated society – somewhat lacking, simply not enough, genetically disadvantaged.

Cats have made a home of the theatre, where young Nana, the eponymous heroine of Émile Zola's 1880 novel, performs the role of Venus. When Count Muffat goes backstage, accompanying the Prince, his senses are overwhelmed, 'breathing in all the animal essence of woman'.[51] He notices the family of cats – a large ginger one and a black female with a litter of black kittens. They seem perfectly at home in this environment, which unsettles the Count greatly – the smells, the heat, the filth, the glimpses of naked flesh. Reading between the lines, the Count seems to see the cats as symbolic of the loose morals which clearly reign in the seedy world of the theatre. But he also observes how comfortable the cats seem to be in this squalor: 'The litter of black kittens were sleeping on the oilcloth, nestling against their mother's belly. She was lying with her paws outstretched, in a state of perfect bliss.'[52] The cats seem to follow their instincts in pursuing happiness and contentment, similar to Nana and the other artistes, who lead a life free of rigid morals. By the end of the chapter, Count Muffat has been seduced by this promise of freedom and pleasure – and, most importantly, by Nana. He is ready to abandon all for one hour of passion with her.

In contrast to the examples cited above, Anne Brontë uses the cat as a metaphor for the capacity for love and affection, or lack thereof, in her novel *Agnes Grey*. Widow Nancy Brown is very fond of 'her gentle friend the cat', who sits with her, 'her long tail half encircling her velvet paws, and her half-closed eyes dreamily gazing on the low, crooked fender'.[53] To Nancy, the true nature of people reveals itself when they interact with her cat. Mr Hatfield cruelly kicks and shoves her feline friend, whereas Mr Weston is gentle and affectionate, eventually even rescuing the cat from being shot by the gamekeeper.

Other writers have viewed cats in a similar fashion to Anne Brontë, but have pondered more on the animal as a symbol of domestic comfort and the home. In *Robinson Crusoe* Daniel Defoe describes how Crusoe manages to rescue not only the ship's dog, but also its two cats. The cats settle in well to their new island life, so much so that one of the two females produces offspring with a wild and anonymous creature on the island. Although Crusoe has to manage the ever-increasing population by culling a number of the animals, he still happily keeps some of them as pets in his home. It is clear that his small menagerie, including his cats, helps him cope with his isolation and loneliness, perhaps by maintaining the illusion of a normal life.

A cat also makes an appearance in the tale of another castaway, namely Jonathan Swift's Gulliver. Staying with the farmer's giant family in the country of Brobdingnag, Gulliver encounters the pet cat in a typically domestic setting, as the family is seated around the dinner table. He is initially frightened of it, much more frightened than he is of the family's dogs, as he perceives the cat to be a 'fierce animal'.[54] His fear demonstrates the new position Gulliver finds himself in – not master of the house but almost a curious pet himself, at the mercy of the other creatures there. Suddenly he is viewing a cosy domestic scene from a different angle.

Having looked at examples of cats serving as metaphors for wanton female behaviour, we now turn to Mino the cat, who makes a few appearances in D.H. Lawrence's *Women in Love*, and represents the male perspective. The grey tom is Birkin's cat, first encountered by Ursula when Birkin asks her to tea in his lodgings. She arrives with some trepidation, hoping for a profession of love, of some indication that their relationship will move forward. But she is disappointed and annoyed to hear Birkin talk about the rejection of love and physical attraction, of wanting to move beyond these traditional concepts. He desires a new type of relationship, 'an equilibrium, a pure balance of two single beings'.[55] At this point, Mino catches their attention as he suddenly darts into the garden, pursuing a stray female cat. He proceeds to cuff her a few times, ensuring she knows who the master in this relationship is. His demeanour exudes superiority and aloofness, which disgusts Ursula. To her, Mino's behaviour is emblematic of all male behaviour – bullying females into submission, wanting to have the upper hand at all times. We can see how Mino reminds her of Birkin's infuriating monologue on what type of relationship he would be willing to tolerate, all the while not considering how Ursula might feel. Mino's actions trigger an angry outburst that sees Ursula bemoan the 'assumption of male superiority'.[56] Whilst Ursula angrily tells Mino off for his behaviour, we later see Hermione, Birkin's other love interest, attempt to charm and gain control over the young cat, much as she attempts to gain influence over Birkin. But, like his master, Mino 'refused to look at her, indifferently avoided her fingers',[57] ascertaining the male superiority yet again.

Other writers have also utilized the cat's physical abilities to convey a sense of the physical presence of male characters. In F. Scott Fitzgerald's *The Great Gatsby* 'the silhouette of a moving cat wavered across the moonlight',[58] drawing Nick Carraway's attention to the figure of Jay Gatsby emerging from the shadows. Like a cat, he silently appears in the moonlit garden, projecting the confidence and ease of the nocturnal feline explorer. The ability of cats to move quietly is also reflected in *Crime and Punishment*, when Dostoevsky uses it several times to describe the soundless movements of characters, including Raskolnikov when he 'would creep down the stairs like a cat and slip out unseen'.[59]

CLASSIC CAT CHARACTERS

Moving away from metaphor and comparison, the literary greats often incorporated cats into their stories. They may appear as companions to the main human characters, or enjoy only brief appearances, but just like their human characters they are capable of evoking strong emotions in the reader.

François, a large tabby, bears silent witness to his human family's struggles in Zola's earlier novel *Thérèse Raquin*. He has a particular connection with old Madame Raquin, who brought him with her from Vernon when the family moved to the Passage du Pont-Neuf in Paris. At the same time, François also provides comfort to Thérèse, as she finds herself in a loveless marriage and a life that seems to offer no true connection with another human being. As soon as Thérèse and Laurent begin their affair, her feelings towards the cat change. She becomes aware of the cat as an observer to their illicit encounters. 'He seemed to be studying them carefully, without blinking, lost in a sort of diabolical ecstasy.'[60] Things go from bad to worse for François after Laurent and Thérèse conspire to murder Camille. In his anguished state, racked by guilt and remorse, Laurent becomes convinced that poor François is set on avenging

Camille. 'This animal must know everything: there were thoughts in its round eyes, the pupils peculiarly dilated.'[61] The cat also seems to side with paralysed Madame Raquin, sitting on her lap and staring at Laurent with his inscrutable green eyes. Eventually, Laurent cannot bear to be watched by François and viciously tosses him out of the window, leaving him to perish from his injuries.

Some cats purr happily through the pages of the classics, others, such as poor François, meet unfortunate ends before the books are over – and at least two 'classic cats' are dead before they even appear. When Constance Chatterley, the 'Lady' of D.H. Lawrence's *Lady Chatterley's Lover*, hears the cries of a child in her garden, she goes to investigate and discovers the gamekeeper Mellors shouting at his daughter, who is in tears. It transpires that Mellors has just shot a cat, 'A poacher, your Ladyship',[62] in front of the poor child. Connie volunteers to take the girl back to her grandmother in order to calm her. It is an early, and awkward, scene between Lady Chatterley and her future lover. But later that day she delivers a message from her husband to Mellors; that is when she sees the gamekeeper stripped to the waist, and from this point on D.H. Lawrence starts to use the word 'loins' with some regularity. The brutality and emotional turmoil that Connie witnesses earlier in the day, for which the unnamed cat must take some credit, leads to the somewhat more carnal feelings she experiences later.

A dead cat is put to more practical use by Huckleberry Finn in *The Adventures of Tom Sawyer* by Mark Twain (and also proves a useful plot device). Tom comes across his friend on a walk to school one morning:

'Hello, Huckleberry!'
'Hello yourself, and see how you like it.'
'What's that you got?'
'Dead cat.'
'Lemme see him, Huck. My, he's pretty stiff. Where'd you get him?'
'Bought him off'n a boy.'
'What did you give?'
'I give a blue ticket and a bladder that I got at the slaughter-house.'
'Where'd you get the blue ticket?'
'Bought it off'n Ben Rogers two weeks ago for a hoop-stick.'
'Say – what is dead cats good for, Huck?'
'Good for? Cure warts with.'[63]

Huck goes into more detail on the process later in the book:

Why, you take your cat and go and get in the grave-yard 'long about midnight when somebody that was wicked has been buried; and when it's midnight a devil will come, or maybe two or three, but you can't see 'em, you can only hear something like the wind, or maybe hear 'em talk; and when they're taking that feller away, you heave your cat after 'em and say, 'Devil follow corpse, cat follow devil, warts follow cat, I'm done with ye!' That'll fetch any wart.[64]

It is not, however, the Devil that the two boys see in the graveyard. Instead they witness a murder there, the dead cat providing the motivation for their midnight excursion, which sets in train the subsequent events of the adventure.

Readers of L.M. Alcott's *Little Women* could be forgiven for thinking, or misremembering, that Jo March first meets Laurie at the New Year's Eve party, where the two dance in secret so that no one can see Jo's scorched dress. It is, after all, a memorable set piece and one that the film adaptations tend to focus on. Their first meeting was actually some time earlier, as Jo explains herself, talking about 'the Laurence boy' at the family Christmas the week before the dance:

> 'Our cat ran away once, and he brought her back, and we talked over the fence, and were getting on capitally, all about cricket, and so on, when he saw Meg coming, and walked off. I mean to know him some day, for he needs fun, I'm sure he does.'[65]

This runaway cat was Mrs Snowball Pat Paw, such a beloved pet of the March sisters that, when she finally vanished for good, she received her own section in *The Pickwick Portfolio*, the newspaper the girls would write on a weekly basis and Jo, of course, would edit.

THE PUBLIC BEREAVEMENT
It is our painful duty to record the sudden and mysterious disappearance of our cherished friend, Mrs. Snowball Pat Paw. This lovely and beloved cat was the pet of a large circle

of warm and admiring friends; for her beauty attracted all eyes, her graces and virtues endeared her to all hearts, and her loss is deeply felt by the whole community.

When last seen, she was sitting at the gate, watching the butcher's cart, and it is feared that some villain, tempted by her charms, basely stole her. Weeks have passed, but no trace of her has been discovered, and we relinquish all hope, tie a black ribbon to her basket, set aside her dish, and weep for her as one lost to us forever.[66]

This is followed by a poetic lament in her honour. It is Beth March, though, who is the real cat-lover in the family, doting upon her cat and kittens, which bring her comfort during her long illness.

A classic novel almost entirely populated by animals is, of course, George Orwell's *Animal Farm*. While no one would suggest the cat plays a major role in the book, on the few occasions it appears it does have an interesting function. We first see the cat when Old Major, the pig, gives his inspirational speech that leads to the rebellion against Jones the farmer. Although she doesn't seem exactly full of revolutionary fervour when she takes her seat:

Last of all came the cat, who looked round as usual, for the warmest place, and finally squeezed herself in between Boxer and Clover; there she purred contentedly throughout Major's speech without listening to a word of what he was saying.[67]

This attitude continues when, a little later, the farm animals vote on whether or not to consider rats as their comrades – 'There were only four dissentients, the three dogs and the cat, who was afterwards discovered to have voted on both sides.'[68] To be fair, she does get her claws out and attacks a cowman at the Battle of the Cowshed, but her only other mention is when she, quite wisely, vanishes from the farm right before Snowball's purges.

Critics are fairly clear on who is represented by each of the key characters in the novel. Old Major is a blend of Marx and Lenin, Snowball is Stalin, Boxer is the proletariat, and so on, but opinion on who the cat is meant to be is more divided. Some suggest she represents the educated classes in Russia at the time – not part of the aristocracy, but not part of the working classes either – that waited to see how the revolution panned out before deciding whom to support. Another suggestion is that she stands for those who were not fully committed to the cause, but not actively against it either. We will never know precisely what Orwell intended, but her brief appearances do matter and the story wouldn't be the same without her.

In *Ulysses*, James Joyce gives voice to a cat without, at any stage, anthropomorphizing it. Leopold Bloom is in the kitchen, pondering breakfast for himself and his wife, Molly, when their cat, hungry too, starts walking 'stiffly round a leg of the table with tail on high' and calls out with a loud *Mkgnao!* It is unsurprising that Joyce, fond of portmanteau words and even making up his own words, would come up

with such a unique version of the more traditional *meow*.
He also adds an increasing sense of urgency that does,
oddly, capture the nature of cats, by including additional *R*s as the pleading continues – *Mrkgnao* and then
Mrkrgnao! These appeals transform into a more satisfied
Gurrhr! when Bloom finally relents and lays down a saucer
of milk for her. The cat's cries also prompt Bloom to reflect
on feline nature:

> They call them stupid. They understand what we say
> better than we understand them. She understands
> all she wants to. Vindictive too. Cruel. Her nature.
> Curious mice never squeal. Seem to like it. Wonder
> what I look like to her. Height of a tower? No, she can
> jump me.[69]

When he returns after a trip to the butcher, with kidneys
for breakfast, Bloom lets the cat lick the blood-smeared
paper and, after he has served the dish to Molly, also gives
the cat some of the scrapings from the pan.

Although this particular feline in literature remains
unnamed, she is permitted a memorable episode, and it is
the only time in the book when Joyce explores the thoughts
and feelings of animals. Other creatures appear, and they
are commented upon, but these are observations of external
actions, not what might be going on inside. And there is a
hint about Joyce's own experience with cats in what might,
at first, appear to be a few seemingly throwaway lines:

> The cat mewed in answer and stalked again stiffly round a leg
> of the table, mewing. Just how she stalks over my writing-
> table. Prr. Scratch my head. Prr.[70]

It doesn't take a huge leap of imagination to believe that
Joyce himself received a few such requests for head scratches
while he was writing *Ulysses*.

Jun'ichirō Tanizaki is one of Japan's most revered
twentieth-century writers, with many of his novels considered classics of Japanese literature. One of his shorter works,
the 1936 novella *A Cat, a Man, and Two Women*, features, as
the title suggests, a feline character at the heart of its plot.

The story opens with a letter from Shinako to her ex-
husband Shozo's new wife, Fukuko, pleading for custody of
Lily. Lily is the cat she and Shozo used to care for together
but which he insisted on keeping after their split. He had,
after all, brought the cat home in the years before his first
marriage and had a particularly strong bond with the animal.
And this is what Shinako slyly plays up in her letter, suggesting that Shozo favours Lily above either of his wives.

Sure enough, Fukuko starts to notice the attention Lily
receives from Shozo:

> 'Now, I'm not going to get jealous over some cat. But you
> insisted I make marinated mackerel because you like it, even
> after I told you I can't stand it myself. Then you hardly touch
> it and give it all to the cat.'[71]

She tells her husband that either the cat goes or she does. As the aftermath of this ultimatum unfolds, the reader discovers the reason for the first marriage break-up, which it would be a shame to reveal here, but suffice to say a subtle comedy ensues and what would usually be considered a love triangle becomes, with the addition of Lily and the battle for her affections, a love... square? Of course, in typical feline fashion, Lily doesn't seem to care who she ends up with. A much-loved book in its home country, this short novel has taken nearly ninety years to find a wide readership in the English-speaking world but has finally done so thanks to a modern translation by Paul McCarthy.

Whether they appear as metaphors and similes, as unnamed felines who flit through a scene, as treasured pets, as instigators of crucial plot points, or even if they have the misfortune to turn up dead, cats have played roles in classic literature for centuries and, as we see elsewhere in this book, continue to do so to this day.

POETIC CATS

I T IS HARD TO PINPOINT THE FIRST APPEARANCE of a cat in poetry, but it seems fair to assume that cats have been inspiring, and perhaps distracting, poets for almost as long as listeners and readers have been captivated by verse. Cats certainly appear throughout the history of poetry, whether they be active participants in stories told in verse, used as metaphors by poets juggling with imagery and meaning, or as the subjects of moving tributes. In this chapter we explore some of the more famous, and less well known, felines that have been captured in iambic pentameter and rhyming structures of all shapes and sizes.

EPIC CATS

There are no mentions of cats in the more famous epic poems of European literature, which would have originated as oral renditions performed by travelling bards, such as Homer's *Odyssey* and *Iliad*, or *Beowulf*, but they are perhaps included, although not named, in the very earliest poems we know about. The epics of *Gilgamesh* and *Atrahasis*, which date from around the eighteenth century BCE in Mesopotamia, include pre-biblical versions of the flood myth, including an ark and the gathering of animals. In the Atrahasis version, preserved on incomplete clay tablets, it is even specified that the animals came in two by two, suggesting that the story of Noah is a later adaptation. Is it unreasonable to suggest that the list of passengers included cats?

The *Mahābhārata*, the Sanskrit epic about the struggle between two groups of cousins in the Kurukshetra War, was composed between the third and first centuries BCE and includes an amusing fable involving those timeless foes, a cat and a mouse. It may well be the earliest appearance of a cat in poetry.

In an ancient forest there grew a banyan tree. In its branches lived a cat named Lomasa, and at its base lived Palita, a small mouse. Parigha, a human hunter, resided nearby and would often set his nets in the forest, hoping to catch animals that climbed down from the trees to eat the bait. One morning, Palita awoke to find some tasty meat left by Parigha and, small enough to avoid the net, he started to feast. He soon noticed three things, however: he was more or less sitting on top of Lomasa, who was caught in the net; a mongoose was approaching along the forest floor; and an owl observed everything from the branch of a tree. Little Palita found himself with a problem on his paws. If he climbed back down from the net, the mongoose would surely eat him. If he stayed where he was, he would be a tasty snack for the owl. Thinking swiftly, he proposed a deal to Lomasa: that he would help the cat escape in return for protection. The cat had little hope of salvation otherwise and so agreed; the mouse climbed beneath his fur and the predators gave up their plans for mouse breakfast.

Palita began to gnaw at the ropes of the net but seemed to be taking a long time doing so and Lomasa became impatient, asking, 'How is it, O amiable one, that thou dost not proceed with haste in thy work? Dost thou disregard me now, having thyself succeeded in thy object? O slayer of foes, do cut these strings quickly. The hunter will soon come here.' But the mouse was no fool. He realized that Lomasa would almost certainly eat him once he was freed, so took his own sweet time nibbling the threads of the net, explaining, 'If thou be freed at an improper time, I shall have to stand in great fear of thee.'[72]

The cat was not exactly thrilled about this, but then he wasn't really in a position to argue. Palita continued to nibble slowly, finally freeing Lomasa just as Parigha hove into view. The cat thanked the mouse, and offered his paw in friendship, only for Palita to reject it, offering a long list of reasons why there is no such thing as friend or foe, with enmity dictated by circumstance. These reasons, which are developed at some length, reflect some of the broader themes of the *Mahābhārata* itself, and the war that is at its heart; but they also set out the basic principles of cat-and-mouse stories for years to come.

POETS AS OBSERVERS

An early example of a poet observing feline nature and mannerisms is 'Pangur Bán', which is believed to date back to the ninth century and was composed at or near Reichenau Abbey by an Irish monk about his pet cat, named White Pangur. *Pangur* was another word for 'fuller': someone who worked in the cloth-making industry, cleaning and removing the impurities from woollen fabrics. In eight four-line stanzas, the poet compares his own scholarly pursuits with the somewhat more basic ones of his cat. It is such a charming examination of human and feline comparisons that we share it here in full, in a translation from the Old Irish by Robin Flower, although readers may also want to seek out the more recent Seamus Heaney version.

I and *Pangur Bán* my cat,
'Tis a like task we are at:
Hunting mice is his delight,
Hunting words I sit all night.

Better far than praise of men
'Tis to sit with book and pen;
Pangur bears me no ill-will,
He too plies his simple skill.

'Tis a merry task to see
At our tasks how glad are we,
When at home we sit and find
Entertainment to our mind.

Oftentimes a mouse will stray
In the hero *Pangur*'s way;
Oftentimes my keen thought set
Takes a meaning in its net.

'Gainst the wall he sets his eye
Full and fierce and sharp and sly;
'Gainst the wall of knowledge I
All my little wisdom try.

When a mouse darts from its den,
O how glad is *Pangur* then!
O what gladness do I prove
When I solve the doubts I love!

So in peace our task we ply,
Pangur Bán, my cat, and I;

In our arts we find our bliss,
I have mine and he has his.

Practice every day has made
Pangur perfect in his trade;
I get wisdom day and night
Turning darkness into light.[73]

This anonymous poet was attempting, with considerable success, to capture a cat in verse, something that countless writers have tried to do in the centuries since, perhaps no one more closely than Christopher Smart. Smart composed his epic religious verse, 'Jubilate Agno', while he was confined at St Luke's Hospital for Lunatics in the late 1750s and early 1760s, reportedly due to 'religious mania'. Each of the poem's 1,200-plus lines begins with either the words 'Let' or 'For'. The 'Let' verses largely compare biblical characters with natural objects; the 'For' verses are more aphoristic in nature and include seventy-four lines about his cat, which lived with him at the hospital. This section of the larger work has become known as 'My Cat Jeoffry'. In it, Smart attributes religious qualities to Jeoffry's daily habits, listing ten of them in particular:

For first he looks upon his forepaws to see if they are clean.
For secondly he kicks up behind to clear away there.
For thirdly he works it upon stretch with the forepaws
    extended.
For fourthly he sharpens his paws by wood.

For fifthly he washes himself.
For sixthly he rolls upon wash.
For seventhly he fleas himself, that he may not be
    interrupted upon the beat.
For eighthly he rubs himself against a post.
For ninthly he looks up for his instructions.
For tenthly he goes in quest of food.[74]

All of which the poet suggests are ways in which Jeoffry
'consider'd God'. Contemporary readers, and those of a less
devout persuasion, may well view these actions as simply the
natural characteristics of every cat they have ever owned or
met, rather than religious ceremony, but Smart's is certainly
a more poetic viewpoint, and he does a wonderful job of
conveying the feline grooming routine. He also has time
for a short jingoistic claim that, 'For the English Cats are
the best in Europe', although quite how he measured this is
unclear from the poem.

Writing only a few years after Smart, William Cowper
offers his own observations on cat behaviour in 'The Retired
Cat', and captures how his pet 'Was much addicted to
inquire / For nooks, to which she might retire, / And where,
secure as mouse in chink, / She might repose, or sit and
think.'[75] The cats of poets are perhaps not all that different to
poets themselves in this regard.

Scottish poet and dramatist Joanna Baillie encapsulates
the vigour and bravado of the younger of the species in her

lengthy poem 'The Kitten', first published in 1810. An early section shows signs of that hunting instinct:

> Backward coil'd and crouching low,
> With glaring eyeballs watch thy foe,
> The housewife's spindle whirling round,
> Or thread or straw that on the ground
> Its shadow throws, by urchin sly
> Held out to lure thy roving eye;
> Then stealing onward, fiercely spring
> Upon the tempting faithless thing.[76]

All of these poems suggest authors who have spent hours observing their feline companions, with curiosity, affection and perhaps more than a little bewilderment. The fact that the cats they write about are instantly recognizable, despite having existed centuries ago, is testament to how well they have been preserved in verse, as well as to the consistent nature of cat behaviour over time.

DEARLY DEPARTED PETS

If poets have been often moved to record the spirit and habits of their cats, it suggests a warm bond between human and animal. It is unsurprising, then, that many poems act as eulogies or tributes to dearly departed pets. Thomas Hardy makes the purpose of 'Last Words to a Dumb Friend' clear from the opening lines: 'Pet was never mourned as you /

Purrer of the spotless hue'. He goes on to share memories of his cat arching its back for a stroke, of having to wipe down chairs to remove cat fur, and of the way the cat would claw at the bark of a tree in the garden. At one point, overcome with grief, he exclaims 'Never another pet for me!' The poem is more than a century old but the scenes and sentiments it contains will resonate with anyone who has owned and loved a cat. The ending is particularly moving:

> Housemate, I can think you still
> Bounding to the window-sill,
> Over which I vaguely see
> Your small mound beneath the tree,
> Showing in the autumn shade
> That you moulder where you played.[77]

Some cats, like Hardy's, die of old age. Others die of misadventure, such as Selima, subject of 'Ode on the Death of a Favourite Cat Drowned in a Tub of Goldfishes' by eighteenth-century poet Thomas Gray, a contemporary of Christopher Smart at Cambridge. This unlucky cat was reclining beside a pond when she spotted flashes of gold. 'She stretched in vain to reach the prize' but 'The slippery verge her feet beguiled, / She tumbled headlong in.'[78] The goldfish may have forgotten Selima seconds after her watery demise but her memory lives on in Gray's tribute.

The eighteenth-century theologian John Jortin took things one step further and pondered the feline afterlife:

The Epitaph of Felis
Who departed this life in the year 1757, at the age of
   14 years, 11 months and 4 days.
I most gentle of cats through long-drawn sickness aweary,
Bidding a last farewell, turn to the waters below.
Quietly smiling to me says Queen Prosperina, 'Welcome!
Thine are the groves of the blest: thine the Elysian suns.'
If I deserve so well, O merciful Queen of the Silent,
Let me come back one night homeward returning again,
Crossing the threshold again in the ear of the master to
   murmur,
'Even when over the Styx, Felis is faithful to thee.'[79]

Christina Rossetti wrote 'On the Death of a Cat' when
she was just 16, and the subtitle, 'A Friend of Mine Aged
Ten years and a Half' suggests the two were companions for
much of the author's life up to that point. 'Of a noble race she
came, / And Grimalkin was her name', and poor Grimalkin
appears to have died during childbirth:

But one night, reft of her strength,
She laid down and died at length:
Lay a kitten by her side,
In whose life the mother died.[80]

A cat doesn't even need to have left for the great cattery
in the sky for poets to eulogize them. Gavin Ewart was
clearly pondering the impending demise when he wrote 'A
14-Year-Old Convalescent Cat in the Winter',[81] wishing

'another living summer' on his pet before the last journey to the vet, from which there is no return. In 'Ghost Cat', Margaret Atwood charts the descent into dementia of one of her pets that started taking bites out of fruit and vegetables, as if she had forgotten what cats are supposed to eat. Atwood has explored the life and death of cats in several of her poems. She receives a long-distance phone call with news that her beloved pet has been put down while she is away, her sister wrapping it in red silk and storing it in the freezer until Margaret can return and bury it herself, in the appropriately titled 'Blackie in Antarctica'. But it is when she explores our relationship with cats, and why their deaths hit us so hard, that she presents one of her most insightful cat poems. 'Mourning for Cats' points out that we rarely, if ever, shed a tear over the death of a spider, crab or fish, but that the passing of a pet cat will bring forth tears of genuine grief. Her suggestion that 'we can no longer see in the dark without them'[82] is a suitably poetic answer.

GOOD CATS, BAD CATS

It is in the nature of cats to hunt, and to kill, as the nineteenth-century German poet and essayist Heinrich Heine hints at in this charming origin story from his longer work, 'Songs of Creation', here translated by Edward Alfred Bowring:

Wild beasts he created later,
Lions with their paws so furious;
In the image of the lion
Made he kittens small and curious.[83]

And the poor mouse is often the prey, which Robert Herrick, probably best known for the line 'Gather ye rose-buds while ye may' from 'To the Virgins, to Make Much of Time', addresses in a number of his poems, nearly two millennia after Lomasa and Palita, and three centuries before Tom and Jerry. From his poem 'A Country Life': 'And the brisk Mouse may feast her self with crumbs / Till that the green-eyed Kitling comes.'[84] And from 'His Grange, or Private Wealth': 'A cat / I keep that plays about my house, / Grown fat / With eating many a miching mouse.'[85]

Some poets have elevated their cats above all other animals. The presence of a cat certainly appears to be an essential requirement for French poet Guillaume Apollinaire, who lists 'A cat moving among the books'[86] as one of just three things he would like in his house, along with a sensible woman and friends that he cannot live without. Pablo Neruda, in 'Ode to the Cat', suggests that cats are the only complete and perfect creatures, which does seem rather biased, but is a view that may be shared by some readers of this book.

These days, vets discourage us from giving cats milk to drink, but – like feeding bread to ducks – humans have long ignored this advice, largely because the recipients seem to like it so much. Harold Munro, the founder of the Poetry Bookshop in Bloomsbury, a mecca for poets and poetry enthusiasts during the 1910s and early 1920s, appears to have been one such flouter of the rules, as his poem 'Milk for the Cat' proves. Munro describes teatime at five o'clock and the agitated cat awaiting its treat, until

> The white saucer like some full moon descends
> At last from the clouds of the table above;
> She sighs and dreams and thrills and glows,
> Transfigured with love.
>
> She nestles over the shining rim,
> Buries her chin in the creamy sea;
> Her tail hangs loose; each drowsy paw
> Is doubled under each bending knee.
>
> A long, dim ecstasy holds her life;
> Her world is an infinite shapeless white,
> Till her tongue has curled the last holy drop,
> Then she sinks back into the night[87]

Not all poets are that keen on cats, though. The Welsh poet W.H. Davies, who spent several years in America as what would then have been called a hobo, was unnerved by the creatures, as he explains in his poem 'The Cat'. The reader can imagine that a quest by the homeless Davies for a sheltered place to sleep inspired these lines:

Within that porch, across the way,
I see two naked eyes this night;
Two eyes that neither shut nor blink,
Searching my face with a green light.

But cats to me are strange, so strange –
I cannot sleep if one is near;
And though I'm sure I see those eyes,
I'm not so sure a body's there![88]

And at least one poet has been so bold as to suggest that cats could be altered for the better. In 'The Cat Improvement Co.', by Brian W. Aldiss, the mysterious company of the title has removed teeth, claws and whiskers from cats, as well as the feline instinct to hunt and kill.

Moreover, the Cat Improvement Co.
Gives with each pet a guarantee:
'Outside bedroom windows it will not yowl;
Also in corners it will not pee'.[89]

The poem signs off with a mischievous hint that human improvements are soon to follow.

The pages of this chapter have so far been populated with the names of famous poets whose work has appeared in esteemed publications. One lesser-known outlet for feline verse we were delighted to discover is *The Cat's Newspaper*, a periodical from the 1880s edited by the 10-year-old son of Dr Richard Garnett. Garnett was, for nearly fifty years, assistant in the Department of Printed Books at the British Museum; his son's newspaper was largely devoted to the goings on of the Garnett family cats and those of their neighbours. We include Dr Garnett's poem to his own cat, Marigold, in tribute to all those amateur poets across the centuries who have, in their own way, tried to capture cats in verse.

Marigold
She moved through the garden in glory, because
She had very long claws at the end of her paws.
Her back was arched, her tail was high,
A green fire glared in her vivid eye;
And all the Toms, though never so bold,
Quailed at the martial Marigold.[90]

Of course, no celebration of cats in literature, and specifically poetry, would be complete without mention of *Old Possum's Book of Practical Cats* by T.S. Eliot, a collection of whimsical rhymes that inspired one of the most successful stage musicals of all time, as well as one of the worst feature films. Eliot originally composed the poems for his godchildren and included them in letters he wrote to them in the 1930s. They appeared in book form at the end of that decade and have remained in print, often accompanied by splendid illustrations, ever since.

While their appeal, especially to younger readers, will still be apparent in the sing-song metre and rhyme, and the amusing names such as Skimbleshanks, Jellicle and

Rumpelteazer, the poems are not without potential problems for a modern audience. Any adult reading them aloud to small children today will have to apply deft censorship when they reach 'Growltiger's Last Stand' in order to avoid some unpleasant racist stereotypes, and the poems are littered with references that will make little sense unless you were raised by a nanny in Central London between the wars.

Eliot does manage to capture the many facets of feline personalities, though, with the Old Gumbie Cat that sleeps all day and plays at night, or Rum Tum Tugger, who wants to be out when you let him in and wants to be back in when you let him out. And then there is Macavity, the ginger Mystery Cat, who, according to Scotland Yard, is responsible, or at least blamed for, a number of crimes including the looting of larders, breaking the glass in greenhouses and even the theft of Foreign Office treaties. His is a verse that can be read aloud without apprehension, even if he does rhyme 'Macavity' with 'suavity'.

The nature of cats is something that poets never seem to tire of exploring – trying to find the words, phrases and imagery to convey their unique qualities and personalities, as well as their lasting bond with humans. This has resulted in millennia of verse – humorous, serious, captivating and moving – and will no doubt continue to do so for as long as poets put pen to paper, or fingertips to keyboard.

BOOKS *for* KITTENS

I F YOU HAVE EVER WITNESSED YOUNG CHILDREN
playing with cats, you know that it can be highly
entertaining – more often than not, the cat will try to escape
the affections of the child, elegantly ducking and weaving
through sticky fingers. If it is a particularly patient and
gracious cat, it might accept its young admirer's affections
for a little while. It is a joy to see how children marvel at the
lovely soft fur, but also hilarious to watch them become more
and more vexed as the clever cat escapes time and time again.

The dynamic changes if it is a kitten and a child playing
together – there often seems to be an instant bond, and the
sheer delight they find in each other becomes apparent as
they devise games to play and eventually collapse into a
purring and giggling pile of pudgy limbs and furry paws.

Children's fascination and, at times, exasperation with cats is reflected in many children's books. Sometimes the cat plays a mere supporting role, but at others it takes the lead, often being given a distinctive voice and a colourful character. The cat's independence, stubbornness, as well as silky beauty and elegance, provide a treasure trove for writers and illustrators, and lend themselves to stories which are funny and exciting in equal measure.

So many books for young readers feature cats in some shape or form that to select only a handful of these is a challenge. This chapter hopes to provide an impression of how both writers and illustrators have been influenced and inspired by cats in their storytelling, exploring some of the most enduring favourites, as well as more recent creations, which celebrate the magic of cats.

FAMILY CATS

Beatrix Potter's stories have entertained generations of children all over the world since she first published a story about four little rabbits in 1901. Today, over 2 million copies of her books are sold across the globe every year. Alongside the likes of Peter Rabbit and Jemima Puddle-Duck, her stories also feature a host of feline characters, accompanied by her trademark illustrations. In *The Tale of Tom Kitten* we meet mother cat Tabitha Twitchit and her three kittens:

Mittens, Tom Kitten and Moppet. Anticipating a visit from her friend, Tabitha attempts to make her three unruly kittens presentable, forcing them into the most uncomfortable and impractical clothes. Tom's horrified facial expression tells us just how unbearable he finds this whole process. Naturally, their mother's warning not to get their outfits dirty is quickly forgotten. One cannot help but find joy in witnessing the kittens, slowly but surely, give in to the temptation of wild and free play, all the while shedding their nice clothes.

We encounter the three siblings again in *The Tale of Samuel Whiskers or The Roly-Poly Pudding*, where mother Twitchit, rather cruelly, wishes to lock the kittens away on baking day, for convenience's sake. She cannot find Tom, who has been hiding in the house's secret nooks and crannies. Poor Tom experiences a childhood trauma when he is captured by rats who want to turn him into a pudding. Luckily, he is eventually saved, although he never forgets his experience and forever remains afraid of rats.

Miss Moppet, Tom's sister, then takes centre stage in *The Story of Miss Moppet*, where she engages in a literal cat-and-mouse game with a small rodent. Both animals come out of the encounter the worse for wear. In all of her kitten stories, Potter chronicles childhood's ups and downs, the lessons one learns through painful, sometimes scary, often funny experiences, perfectly capturing the young creatures' energy and emotions in her illustrations – and each recreates a scenario that is probably familiar to both the human grown-ups and the children who, more than a century later, still read these tales together.

Kathleen Hale also chose to give her creations human voices in her classic picture book series about Orlando the Marmalade Cat. The illustrator and writer published the first book, *A Camping Holiday*, in 1938, followed by eighteen further books. Her vivid and colourful illustrations portray Orlando and his family, consisting of wife Grace and three kittens, 'the Tortoiseshell Pansy, snow-white Blanche and coal-black Tinkle', in all their furry glory.[91] The cats are undeniably true felines, with a love of fish and Orlando's profession of catching mice, but at the same time Hale lets them exhibit some very human habits and traits with a feline twist. Orlando proudly carries a wristwatch – but on his tail. Intent on sharing news of their camping holiday with friends at home, they send postcards – but the stamps insist on getting stuck on their whiskers. The cat characters come to life on the page, particularly the sometimes mischievous kittens, and it is easy to understand why Hale's books were such a long-lasting success with young readers.

More recently, we have Judith Kerr to thank for one of the most beloved cat characters in children's fiction today – Mog. The first of over twenty books featuring this rather splendid creature was published in 1970. *Mog the Forgetful*

Cat introduced young readers to the lovable and exasperating cat, who shares her home with the Thomas family. The first pages of the book establish that Mog is 'nice but not very clever'[92] and, as the title suggests, very forgetful, which can be quite annoying at times for her owners. But, whereas Mr Thomas looks unhappy about Mog's shenanigans, daughter Debbie is much more gracious and forgives Mog's short-comings, as she is such a nice cat.

Kerr's expressive and colourful drawings certainly convey that Mog is indeed a lovely cat – round and fluffy, with beautiful fur and eyes. This first story establishes a pattern, which appears across the series, of Mog annoying her owners, even Debbie at times, but ultimately redeeming herself, if rather more accidentally than intentionally. The many Mog stories see her meet a very noisy baby, do a horrible thing on Mr Thomas's favourite chair and wreak havoc at the vet, among other escapades, but somehow always managing to find a happy ending to her madcap adventures. Kerr admitted that her Mog stories were inspired by the actions of her own family cats and it is apparent that she paid close attention to feline behaviour as she perfectly portrays the often wilful, occasionally a little spiteful, sometimes very loving behaviour of cats which makes them such compelling pets. In 2002 Kerr published the final and most moving Mog story. In *Goodbye Mog*, she acknowledges that family cats cannot stay with you forever, as much as we would like them to. Mog peacefully goes to sleep and never wakes up again, 'But a little bit of her stayed awake'[93] to find out what the Thomas family would do next. When they eventually acquire a new kitten, Mog's ghost graciously lends it a helping paw, showing her successor the right kind of feline behaviour. In an interview at the time of publication, Kerr reflected on how children quite often encounter death in their young lives, for example when their pets pass away. She felt that it was appropriate and right to acknowledge this in her final Mog story. In 2015, to everyone's surprise and delight, Mog was briefly brought back to life for a highly successful supermarket advert, and the book tie-in provided Kerr with her first number-one UK bestseller, at the age of 92, showing how popular this particular feline continues to be.

Kerr produced another homage to cats, in the shape of *Katinka's Tail*. It was inspired by the ninth in a long line of pet cats, who sported a tail which looked as if it belonged to a different animal. The story focuses on a woman (who closely resembles Kerr) and her cat, Katinka. It is a testament to the everyday companionship of cats, and the typical activities cats and their owners undertake together. But it also explores the mysterious night-time adventures of cats, when they leave cosy domesticity behind and, to some extent, return to the feral nature of their ancestors. The story hints at the magical powers that have been assigned to the cat throughout history. Ultimately, the eponymous tail and its abilities remind us how a pet cat can hold a very special place in their owner's heart.

The mystery of a cat's nocturnal escapades is also the subject of Lynley Dodd's beautifully illustrated *Slinky Malinki Catflaps*. As the name suggests, we are able to follow the cat Slinky Malinki as he squeezes through his catflap and ventures out into the night. Here, he meets his ragtag gang of feline friends, and together they go on the prowl. A dramatic encounter with their arch enemy, Scarface Claw, leads to hair-raising caterwauling, harking back to the images of demonic cats haunting the night, depicted in an image of raised tails and fierce eyes.

PICTURING FELINES

Kerr's and Dodd's cat tales are perfect examples of the advantage illustrated children's books hold – namely the ability to provide a visual image of the cat's characteristics and qualities. The cat's facial expressions and posture convey a range of emotions, from delight to shame, contentment to anger. Through images and words, young readers can easily relate to what the cats experience – in Mog's case, the challenges of dealing with new experiences and navigating relationships with our nearest and dearest, or, in the case of Slinky Malinki and his crew, the excitement of being with your friends and sharing in secret adventures before going back to the safe haven of home.

Writer Kes Gray, and illustrator Jim Field, have featured a host of different animals in their series of rhyming *Oi!* books, among them also the cat. In *Oi, Cat!* the titular feline engages in a silly rhyming word battle with a frog and a dog, as they debate what object (or animal) the cat is allowed to sit on. Their cat is pictured with a perpetual frown and down-turned mouth. The story does not progress according to the cat's wishes and, most annoyingly, its chagrin is caused by a dog, of all creatures. The cat's grim face expresses its displeasure with the world – until the end of the tale. As cats are wont to do, the grumpy cat eventually boasts an evil grin as it manages to turn the situation to its advantage, and to the dog's disadvantage.

The now classic series of books featuring the witch Meg and her cat Mog include very distinctive and vibrant illustrations, instantly recognizable to generations of readers who grew up with their stories. Written by Helen Nicoll and illustrated by Jan Pieńkowski, Mog's black-and-white striped body is pleasingly pear-shaped, with a curling tail, pointy ears and, most importantly, big yellow eyes. The illustrations reflect how fascinated humans are by the cat's ability to move with such ease and grace, as well as by the extraordinary shape of cats' eyes, which are so unlike the human eye.

These eyes and the constantly moving tail express much of Mog's emotions, be it excitement, shock or exasperation, as yet another of Meg's spells has unintended consequences. Rather than being a mere accessory to the witch, Mog acts as a companion and conspirator in their adventures, making suggestions and asking questions, expressing her own ideas, dreams and wishes.

Quirky watercolour illustrations of cats appear regularly in the work of Japanese author and illustrator Satoshi Kitamura, across books for children of all ages. In the board book *Cat is Sleepy* a clearly rather fatigued feline stares out with heavy eyelids from the cover. Inside its handful of pages, he attempts to find a place to sleep, not always with great success. It is an ideal 'one more book before bedtime' story for parents eager to get their children to sleep.

As children get older they can enjoy increasingly surreal picture books by Kitamura, including the award-winning *Me and My Cat*, in which a woman with a pointy hat and a broomstick puts a magic spell on Nicholas. The next morning he discovers he has swapped places with his pet cat, Leonardo. At first, the boy is baffled and a little scared, but he soon realizes the potential benefits of his situation – 'Maybe it wasn't such a bad thing to be a cat? I didn't have to go to school, did I?' – and he starts to explore the neighbourhood, which is very different from a feline perspective. However, after fighting with some other cats, and being chased by a dog, he decides that 'life was as tough and complicated as it was for humans'.[94] Leonardo's exploits are enjoyable to watch, but even more fun is seeing Nicholas attempt to come home from school via the catflap and eat his meals from the cat bowl. After a most peculiar day that has caused much consternation for Nicholas's mother, the woman with the pointy hat returns to declare: 'Sorry, love, I got the wrong address.' The next morning everything has returned to normal for Nicholas, although when he gets to school his teacher is acting most unusually, an ending to prompt knowing smiles from readers no matter what their age.

Kitamura's most famous creation, though, is Boots, a ginger tom who is the star of numerous stories and appears in board books, picture books and even comic books for older readers. Although the stories and readership may change, Boots's quizzical expressions and alternative take on the world around him are consistent throughout. It is good to think that children can grow up with Boots, reading him at various stages in their lives. He is such a beloved character that in 2006 he appeared on a special edition 42 pence postage stamp.

CAT COMPANIONS

Companionship and friendship are common themes among many children's books featuring cats. Popular culture often identifies the dog as humankind's loyal companion and it is therefore intriguing to see so many stories for younger readers portray a close bond between a child and the ultimate independent spirit, a cat.

A deep and lasting human–feline friendship is at the core of Sven Nordqvist's *Pettson and Findus* books. Pettson is an old farmer who lives in a picturesque red house in the Swedish countryside with only his chickens for company. One day his neighbour brings him a box containing a small kitten – Findus. Together, Pettson and Findus share in the simple pleasures in life – eating pancakes, going fishing, playing in the snow. Findus is not so much a graceful and aloof cat, but instead takes on the role of a child, emphasized by his distinct clothing, consisting of green trousers and a green hat, as well as his habit of walking on his hind legs. Findus occasionally causes mayhem, but he also challenges Pettson to enjoy life to the full. Their shared adventures show us that we all need a true friend and that friendship comes in all shapes and sizes. They are also a wonderful testament to the beautiful dynamic that can often emerge between old and young – helping and inspiring each other.

Another engaging feline companion is Mr Pusskins, friends with a young girl named Emily. They feature in a series of picture books created by Sam Lloyd. The bold illustrations portray Mr Pusskins as a passionate animal, in contrast to his cuddly name. In *Mr Pusskins: Best in Show* his owner Emily wants to show off the, in her eyes, most handsome cat in a pet show. Although Mr Pusskins is initially less than willing, his competitiveness and ambition soon get the better of him, particularly because there is a trophy to be won. Despite these less-endearing attributes, Emily still cherishes Mr Pusskins and firmly believes in him.

In Emily Gravett's *Matilda's Cat*, the cat in question does not enjoy the many activities and games the little girl Matilda would like to involve her in. The cat's features express lack of interest or disapproval, at times even fear. All the time the reader wonders why the little girl, who even dresses in a furry costume which makes her look like the cat, seems to love her cat so much. We discover the reason on the final page – because the one thing the cat does love is Matilda.

How such affection between a child and a very independent cat might develop is explored in Charlotte Voake's *Ginger Finds a Home*. We meet Ginger when he is merely a stray cat, sleeping in a patch of weeds, drinking from puddles and searching for food every day – until a little girl begins to take notice of him, slowly and patiently winning his confidence and affection. Although Ginger is neither particularly beautiful nor clever, the girl has chosen him and pours all her efforts into convincing him that he is safe with her.

A true partnership lies at the centre of Julia Donaldson's *Tabby McTat*, illustrated by Axel Scheffler. Tabby is a feline performer, busking on the streets with her human friend Fred, lending his unique (and loud) voice to their favourite song. The song expresses how '*PURRRR-fectly happy*'[95] they are with each other. But one day Tabby is distracted by the beautiful Sock and unintentionally loses sight of Fred. Tabby joins Sock in her home where they eventually have three kittens, but he never forgets his good friend Fred. When they are finally reunited, Tabby realizes that he does not want to abandon Sock and the comforts of home for a busker's life, but luckily one of his kittens is a talented singer and decides to join Fred in its father's place. Ironically, the cat in this story is more of a homebody than the human, despite the independence and sense of adventure we often associate with cats.

Nick Sharratt's *The Cat and the King* also depicts a companionship between its two main characters. Sharratt's illustrations show a cat with a friendly facial expression, but with a human-like body, standing on its hind legs. The cat in this story holds a definite advantage over its human. Tibbles the cat manages the King's life, expertly using a laptop and even holding a driving licence. When the King loses his castle, and with it his royal lifestyle, he is forced to move into a normal house in a normal neighbourhood. Frequently baffled by the mechanics of everyday life, he completely relies on Tibbles to provide food and shelter. Tibbles is a gracious and kind cat, who cares very much about maintaining an illusion of royal privilege for the King, whilst also gently nudging him to accept and cope with their new life.

We recognize the independence of other feline characters, but the cat's selflessness seems unusual in comparison to the stereotypically selfish cat behaviour.

Whilst these stories show us what brilliant friends cats can be, children's writers have also explored the more roguish nature of cats, much to the delight of their young readers.

The ultimate mischief-filled fictional feline surely has to be Dr Seuss's *The Cat in the Hat*. The cat appears when needed most – when the boy narrator of the book and his sister Sally are stuck at home, under strict instructions to behave until their mother returns. Their only company is a rather stern, talking pet fish. Every child knows the feeling of intense boredom so well – and which child would not want a magical talking cat to appear suddenly and provide some entertainment? And which parent does not ponder the mysterious activities children get up to when no adults are watching? As we have seen, the same also applies to cats – they tend to disappear for hours on end and nobody knows exactly what they do and whom they meet. In typical Seussian fashion, the story takes these everyday situations and thoughts to the extreme. Although he seems to have the best intentions, the cat creates utter mayhem. He balances precariously on a ball, juggling books, cake and a fish bowl among other things. But, of course, he comes down 'with a bump',[96] making a mess in the process. In his attempt to win over the ever-critical pet fish, who wants the cat to leave immediately, he introduces Thing One and Thing Two. These two creatures seem very friendly but their endeavours to entertain the children bring further chaos. Although the cat seems to make the situation increasingly worse and the fish becomes more and more agitated, the wily cat ultimately proves that he is a good feline and ensures that the children do not get into trouble. First published in 1957, *The Cat in the Hat* has become a modern classic and continues to sell hundreds of thousands of copies every year, in multiple languages, proving the continuing appeal of the naughty but fun cat.

Chris Riddell's distinctive and intricate illustrations suit the feline character in his book *Ottoline and the Yellow Cat* perfectly. The cat in question is tall and elegant, her long limbs well suited to her profession of – what else? – cat burglar. She is the ideal criminal mastermind: mysterious and devious, an orchestrator of evil plans. Riddell seems to hint at the cat's superiority over dogs by putting her in charge of a gang of dogs, which she expertly manages to assist in her criminal endeavours.

As we move on to stories for older children, the relationships between cats and humans become more complex and writers explore the cat's multifaceted personality in their storytelling. These novels often touch on the mythical past of the cat, emphasizing the animal's mysterious nature and extraordinary capabilities.

CAT MAGIC

The long-held belief that cats have a connection with devils and demons, as explored in our first chapter, works to the advantage of the eponymous protagonist of Neil Gaiman's novel *Coraline*. As the young girl has to navigate a world created by an evil creature, a black cat comes to her assistance in the quest to undo some of the spirit's dark deeds. Conveniently, the cat holds important knowledge about the creature, providing Coraline with useful hints and tips. The cat displays stereotypical sarcasm and disdain – when Coraline suggests that they could be friends, the cat counters that they also '*could* be rare specimens of an exotic breed of African dancing elephants'.[97] But despite its knowledge of the dark world Coraline finds herself in, it is not of an evil nature. It appears that the cat is the only character who is not spellbound by the spirit, suggesting perhaps that feline independence protects the cat from its influence.

A slightly friendlier and also very helpful cat appears in Sally Gardener's *Wings & Co.* series, illustrated by David Roberts. Fidget, the talking cat, walks on his hind legs, provides excellent advice and a seemingly endless supply of comfort food. He helps 11-year-old Emily run the Wings & Co. detective agency and takes on an almost parental role, exuding cool and calm when various magic beings create havoc.

In *His Royal Whiskers*, Sam Gayton also alludes to an affinity between cats and magic. At 6 years old, Alexander, Prince of Petrossia and son of the bloodthirsty czar, is turned into a kitten of, eventually, huge proportions, after drinking a potion concocted by his two friends, Pieter and Teresa. The juxtaposition of a fluffy, albeit very large, kitten and its role in reprimanding his cruel bully of a father hints at the stubborn and independent character of cats.

In Jill Murphy's *The Worst Witch*, the most magical of human–cat relationships is explored as young witch Mildred Hubble receives the typical feline witch's familiar, distributed in an official ceremony at Miss Cackle's Academy for Witches. Unfortunately, there are no black kittens left when it is Mildred's turn – instead, she is left with a tabby with white paws. Tabby the cat resembles Mildred to some extent – both are clumsy and a little different to the other witches and cats. Hence, they form an unbreakable friendship, supporting each other through hair-raising trials and tribulations.

The classic tale of *Carbonel: King of Cats*, written by Barbara Sleigh, introduces us to another witch's cat. The central human character of the story is Rosemary, a girl who lives in London with her mother. Through a few twists and turns, Rosemary acquires an old broom and a rather lovely black cat from a strange old lady. She soon realizes that this old lady was indeed a witch and that the black cat is a true witch's familiar. He goes by the name of Carbonel. Rosemary can speak to him, but only when holding the broomstick. Carbonel immediately makes it clear that he is no 'common or garden, mousing, sit-by-the-fire cat'; he is a royal cat who is determined to reclaim his throne from the alley cats.[98] Carbonel is knowledgeable about magic, instructing Rosemary on how to fly a broomstick and concoct magic potions. But he is also a true feline, relishing the hidden worlds that only cats can access. He claims that 'it is on the rooftops that we are our true selves. There we live our secret lives, there we skirmish, we royster, we sing songs.'[99]

So far, we have encountered a number of feline characters in children's novels who are closely linked to mythical and magical worlds. In *My Life as a Cat*, Carlie Sorosiak exaggerates the strange and unexpected even more. The feline in question is, in fact, an alien. Hailing from a distant planet, where he forms part of a hive mind, he journeys to Earth to experience life as a human for a limited period of time. But the plan goes awry and instead he lands on planet Earth in the shape of a cat. Soon, a girl called Olive adopts him and names him Leonard. A true friendship develops from here, told from Leonard's perspective, with the benefit of an outsider's view on humankind. Despite his usual existence as one part of a larger entity, the feline shape seems to suit Leonard perfectly. His tendency to observe in wonder seems natural to humans, as cats are prone to silent observation with an expression of intelligence and curiosity. Olive, herself an outsider and often called weird by her peers, confides in Leonard, the silent and attentive listener. Their strong connection eventually leads to some surprising plot developments. Choosing a cat as the host of an alien mind seems a perfect fit – as we found out in the first chapter, cats have extraordinary abilities that baffle humans, much like we imagine aliens would do.

Some writers have indeed taken up the challenge of attempting to imagine what the world might look like through the eyes of these strange creatures.

CAT'S-EYE VIEWS

In stories written from the perspective of cats, the human reader is given unique insight into how our feline companions might view this world. S.F. Said's *Varjak Paw* manages just that in quite an extraordinary way. The titular main character is a Mesopotamian Blue (a breed which, in fact, does not exist) and the reader perceives the world through his eyes. His feline senses make the experience so much more intense than our human perception could ever allow us to. The magical and mythical aspects of the story, which slowly unfold, remind us of the natural instincts and skills which led cats to be connected to deities in Ancient Egypt and which we can sometimes forget when sharing our home with a pet cat. Varjak breaks free of human ownership and embarks on an extraordinary adventure to free his family from the clutches of a sinister man and his terrifying black cats. Along the way, he receives help from his ancestor Jalal, who comes to Varjak in his dreams, teaching him about the Way. The Way describes a set of skills, passed on from generation to generation in Varjak's family, which will hopefully help Varjak defeat the mysterious new enemy and set his family free.[100]

In a similar vein, the long-running *Warriors* series, which has inspired several subseries, also chooses to view the world from the perspective of its feline characters. The first book, *Into the Wild*, introduces us to domestic cat Rusty, who encounters a host of feral cats living in the woods surrounding his humans' house. These cats live in large clans and there is a fragile peace between the different factions. Rusty is eventually accepted into the ThunderClan, one of four feline clans battling for territory. The language used fully embraces the cat point of view, using terms such as 'twoleg' instead of human, 'kittypet' instead of domesticated cat. Spring is referred to as 'newleaf' and winter as 'leafbare', whilst the Milky Way becomes the 'Silverpelt', which is home to the heavenly warriors, or 'StarClan'. The cat characters do not talk; they mew. The reader soon learns more about the myths and legends that form the foundation of this feline society and its complex social hierarchy. A fast-paced plot mirrors the quick reflexes and heightened senses of its central characters – we are immediately immersed in the world of the clans, with vivid descriptions of smells, tastes and visuals. In fact, the 'twolegs' are only relevant to the feline society inasmuch as their machines and lifestyle form a threat to the natural habitat of the clans – we, the readers, become part of the cat warrior society and quickly forget about our human point of view.[101]

German children's writer Michael Ende (author of *The Neverending Story* among others) created another feline character who critically observes the effect humans have on the world in *The Night of Wishes: Or the Satanarchaeolide-alcohellish Notion Potion*.[102] Mauricio di Mauro is a slightly obese tom who lives as the spoilt pet of the aptly named wizard Beelzebub Preposteror. Mauricio has carefully created a persona which stands in stark contrast to his true origin. Born a common street cat called Moritz, he was sent to spy on the wizard by the High Council of the Animals, who rightly suspect Beelzebub of committing terrible ecological crimes on behalf of the Minister of Pitch Darkness (aka the Devil). Seizing the opportunity to start a new life, Moritz became Mauricio, a cat of noble Neapolitan descent who tragically lost his beautiful singing voice. Moritz/ Mauricio soon forgot about his secret mission, seduced by a life of luxury which his master cannily provides, lulling Mauricio into a false sense of security. Beelzebub quickly sees through the cat's story and decides to convince Mauricio he is doing good deeds, rather than trying to destroy the planet. Mauricio buys into the tale and now hero-worships the cunning sorcerer. For good measure, Beelzebub continues to overfeed, as well as regularly sedate Mauricio, keeping him pliable and quiet. Ende's writing wonderfully portrays Mauricio's sheer pathos, dramatic tendencies and self-absorption – traits which we can easily recognize in everyday cat behaviour. But before the reader has a chance to become too exasperated with Mauricio's general uselessness, his life is turned upside down by a new arrival. The raven Jacob Scribble was sent on a similar spying mission by the Council, his target being Beelzebub's aunt and partner in crime, the witch Tyrannia Vampirella. Savvy Jacob knows the two evil geniuses for who they are and Mauricio soon has to admit that he was tricked. All Mauricio now wants to do is make up for his previous failings and stop Beelzebub and Tyrannia from using the Notion Potion to wreak havoc on the natural world, with the help of his new friend Jacob. The little cat plucks up what courage he has and devises a hair-raising plan to finally fulfil his mission and become the noble hero he so longs to be. Now we can finally recognize the other feline traits: stubbornness, determination and a healthy dose of scepticism when it comes to the human capacity to make sensible decisions. Michael Ende not only creates a colourful and, despite his shortcomings, charming character in Mauricio; he also lets both animals speak up for the natural world, which suffers from the pact humanity seems to have made with the Devil. This novel is both an entertaining adventure story and a tale of our time, for readers of all ages who like to think that evil forces set to destroy the planet might eventually be defeated by less powerful, but clever and passionate, creatures.

Whilst these stories fully embrace the cat perspective, there are others, of course, which stay firmly in the human world but assign the feline characters an important role. Cats are often used as vehicles to progress stories, particularly because their independent spirit naturally empowers them to take action and change the course of events.

CAT INTUITION

In Michael Morpurgo's *Kaspar, Prince of Cats* we are transported to London's Savoy Hotel in the early twentieth century. Bellboy Johnny Trott meets Kaspar, named 'the prince of cats'[103] by his owner, the Countess Kandinsky, a guest at the hotel. When she unexpectedly dies, Johnny decides to take care of the beautiful cat. His new companion leads him to tackle adventures and forge new friendships, eventually seeing him travel to America on the doomed *Titanic*. Kaspar motivates Johnny to take charge of his life, to take risks and seize opportunities. In this story, the cat brings people together, providing a bond between individuals who would usually have never formed friendships. Kaspar's character was inspired by the eponymous sculpture in the hotel's restaurant, used to round up unlucky dinner parties of thirteen guests. Morpurgo encountered the sculpture and its story when he was writer-in-residence at the hotel.

The famous Cheshire Cat in Lewis Carroll's *Alice's Adventures in Wonderland* doesn't so much actively intervene in Alice's story but provides brief interludes and a sense of calm during her mind-boggling experiences. When they first meet, Alice asks the cat for advice as to where to go next. In response, the Cheshire Cat provides probably the most accurate and honest description of Alice's surroundings:

> 'What sort of people live about here?'
>
> 'In THAT direction,' the Cat said, waving its right paw round, 'lives a Hatter: and in THAT direction,' waving the other paw, 'lives a March Hare. Visit either you like: they're both mad.'
>
> 'But I don't want to go among mad people,' Alice remarked.
>
> 'Oh, you can't help that,' said the Cat: 'we're all mad here. I'm mad. You're mad.'
>
> 'How do you know I'm mad?' said Alice.
>
> 'You must be,' said the Cat, 'Or you wouldn't have come here.'[104]

Everyone is mad in Wonderland and therefore rational choices and decisions matter very little. John Tenniel's original illustrations depict the cat's famous grin, exuding a typically feline sense of content and self-satisfaction. The Cheshire Cat seems to be the only creature not intimidated by the Queen's constant threat of execution, again displaying the cat's characteristic aloofness, stubbornness and independence, which we have encountered in so many stories already.

Crookshanks, Hermione Granger's cat in J.K. Rowling's *Harry Potter* series, also has a will of his own. Hermione is the first person to bear affection towards him, as nobody else wanted to purchase him as a pet. It speaks of Hermione's belief that every creature deserves to be treated with respect and her seemingly boundless empathy. Crookshanks rewards Hermione's loyalty and affection when he plays a key role in the grand finale of *The Prisoner of Azkaban*. He uses his strong will and ability to recognize someone's true nature to defend Sirius Black and uncover the Animagus Peter Pettigrew.

In Philip Pullman's *His Dark Materials* series, cats play a particular role in Will Parry's life. His cat, Moxie, puts a chain of events in motion, including a man's death, which force him to flee from his Oxford home and his world. Although Will is devastated by having killed a man and consequently having to leave his mother behind, these events ultimately lead him to Lyra, a young girl from an alternative version of Oxford in another dimension where humans are partnered by animal daemons – their spirits in physical form.

His flight is helped by a tabby cat that shows him the window to another world. This cat continues to play a significant role in the story, leading Will and Lyra to make certain decisions and follow a particular path. Will's character chimes with the image we have of cats: he is independent and fierce, but also deeply cares about the people close to him. It is therefore of little surprise when his daemon is eventually revealed and settles as a beautiful, large cat.

A cat also forms part of the cast of recurring characters in the *Hunger Games* series, written by Suzanne Collins. The best-selling books are set in a dystopian future version of the United States, which has been split into thirteen Districts and is ruled by the elite residing in the Capitol. Each year, Districts have to send boys and girls as tributes to compete in the Hunger Games – a fight to the death between all competitors, with only one winner emerging alive at the end. The story follows Katniss Everdeen, one of the tributes, as she first battles for survival in the Hunger Games and eventually takes on the Capitol's ruling elite in an attempt to overthrow the regime which has brought so much pain and grief to the Districts. The unsuitably named Buttercup is the rather ugly but much-loved pet cat of Katniss Everdeen's sister, Primrose, or Prim. He appears on the very first page, where Katniss describes him as 'the world's ugliest cat'.[105] Although Katniss and Buttercup at first do not see eye to eye, they share their love for Prim. Buttercup challenges Katniss to acknowledge her own emotions, not least her devastation at the loss, later in the series, of her sister. Together they mourn Prim, bringing comfort to each other in their grief. The cat gives Katniss a chance to let emotions shine through, when she has to spend much of her time repressing her feelings to deal with the challenges she encounters.

The latter stories are aimed at readers who are on the cusp of adulthood and it seems significant that the cats in these stories are often deeply connected to the young adults' innermost thoughts, hopes and fears. The cats help the human characters cope with difficult situations and feelings, and even to make the right decisions. The theme of friendship between feline and young human from the earlier stories continues, if in more complex events.

This small selection of stories for young readers, from picture books to novels, hints at the appeal that the cat as a character holds for children and young people. As cuddly, lovable and adorable as cats may be, they can also be fiercely independent, mischievous and, at times, even ferocious. But, despite their independent spirit, they also show loyalty to their human companions and express a real sense of belonging. Children often find themselves on a similar journey – looking for love and affection, but simultaneously striving to forge their own path in the world, seeking adventures and independence. All they need is the knowledge that they can return home after a magical adventure.

TALKING CATS

CATS ARE OFTEN PERCEIVED AS MYSTERIOUS creatures – their deep connection with religion, myths and legends, their independent roaming, their inscrutable faces make us ponder what secrets these animals might be hiding. This notion can inspire great stories, as writers attempt to imagine what adventures, trials and tribulations cats might encounter when we, the humans, are not looking. Sometimes, storytellers will go so far as to attempt to recreate the feline perspective and voice, allowing the reader the privilege of seeing the world from their point of view.

There are a plethora of stories where the cat is the narrator, where our human language is used to develop a unique feline voice. Sometimes the human characters are able to understand the cats; sometimes only the reader is given privileged access to the feline interior monologue; and on at least one notable occasion a cat is supposed to have written the book himself.

With his short story 'The Cat that Walked by Himself', Rudyard Kipling created an origin story which neatly sums up the cornerstones of the human–feline relationship. He takes us back to a time where animals were wild and untamed, and humans lived in caves. In the first paragraph, Kipling establishes the unique nature of the cat, for 'the wildest of all the wild animals was the Cat. He walked by himself, and all places were alike to him.'[106] But soon the cat observes curious developments: the woman sharing a cave with the man begins to entice wild animals into becoming domesticated; cleverly, she discovers what it is that each animal most desires that only humans can provide and she agrees a trade with them. The first to succumb to the bargain is the dog. The woman asks him to become her man's companion and guardian and in return she will give him roasted meat and bones. And so it continues with the horse and the cow. The cat immediately understands the woman's game and prides himself on the fact that he cannot be tricked and charmed. But eventually he does become interested in the comforts the human way of life has to offer – a warm fire and delicious milk.

Hence, he and the woman engage in a playful argument in which both of them display humour, wit and cunning. The woman teases the cat, reminding it: 'You are neither a friend nor a servant. You have said it yourself', hence denying the cat access to her homely cave. But the cat knows how to play this game and appeases the woman by shamelessly flattering her and appealing to her good nature: 'You are very wise and very beautiful. You should not be cruel even to a Cat.'[107] Both woman and cat acknowledge each other's cleverness, but each of them believes they can trick the other one. They strike up a bargain: if the woman ever praises the cat, she will allow him certain privileges. It is clear that she does not see the cat as an animal that can fulfil a purpose, such as the dog or cow. But soon she is proved wrong, when her baby finds delight and comfort in the cat's soft fur and playfulness, and when the cat catches rodents in the cave.

The woman admits that the cat has earned his privileges, to sit by the fire and drink milk, which satisfies the cat greatly. When man and dog return at the end of the day, they make it clear that no bargain was struck with them and that the cat will only be tolerated in the cave if he fulfils his purpose as vermin hunter. The cat remains obstinate, stressing that no one controls him – 'still I am the Cat who walks by himself, and all places are alike to me'. His stubbornness annoys both man and dog, and here Kipling very neatly establishes the stereotype of men and canines only barely tolerating cats in their vicinity. Man and dog swear to chase the cat away whenever it is near them, no matter how useful or kind it is. Hence, from there on 'three proper Men out of five will always throw things at a Cat whenever they meet him, and all proper Dogs will chase him up a tree'.[108] The voice which Kipling gives the cat encapsulates both the feline cunning as well as independence – no matter how settled and domesticated we might deem a cat, it will still insist on roaming free and maintaining at least some of its wild and untamed nature.

Angela Carter's reinterpretation of the classic 'Puss-in-Boots' is similar to the original story, in that it celebrates the clever feline nature and disparages the not-so-clever humans, who have to rely on the cat to sort out their lives. But in Carter's version the cat, Figaro, is a foul-mouthed streetwise trickster. He struts the streets, proudly displaying his orange fur, his attention-rousing voice and, of course, his leather boots. Carter's first novel, written when she was just 6 years old, featured cats, and as an adult she also wrote books for children with cat protagonists. She once claimed, 'I get on well with cats because some of my ancestors were witches.' In this story, however, she explores the duplicity we sometimes sense in cats – 'So all cats have a politician's air; we smile and smile and so they think we're villains.'

Figaro settles in with a young and feckless cavalry officer, two rascals forming a partnership that sees them gamble, steal and cheat. When times are good, the master feeds him 'excellent beef sandwich' and 'a snifter of brandy'. But Puss sticks with the new master even when times are hard and 'when the cupboard was as bare as his backside' (the master's backside, rather than the cat's). He witnesses the cavalry officer's many amorous pursuits, making 'the beast with two backs with every harlot in the city'.[109] That is until his master falls in love with a young woman, who is closely guarded and kept locked away by her indifferent husband. Figaro devises a plan to help the two lovebirds not only come together for a few hours of passion, but also to rid themselves of the old husband and live happily ever after on his sizable fortune. As part of his plan, he strikes up a relationship with a kitchen cat, employed in the house of the young lady. After a 'few firm thrusts of [his] striped loins',[110] they are quite comfortable with each other and his new love interest helps him bring the two young people together. Figaro closes the account of his ingenious feat by wishing the reader that 'all your wives, if you need them, be rich and pretty; and all your husbands, if you want them, be young and virile; and all your cats as wily, perspicacious and resourceful as: PUSS-IN-BOOTS'.[111]

ANTISOCIAL CATS

The dangers, rather than the potential benefits, of a talking cat are exposed by Saki (H.H. Munro) in 'Tobermory'. The titular cat becomes the centre of attention of Lady Blemley's house party, when her guest Mr Cornelius Appin claims that he has taught the feline to speak in the human tongue. According to Appin, he tried and failed to teach various other animals but found that he eventually focused solely on cats, 'which have assimilated themselves so marvellously with our civilisation while retaining all their highly developed feral instincts'.[112] He allegedly discovered in Tobermory a highly intelligent feline. The other guests do not believe him, until Tobermory proves them wrong by starting to speak in a highly sophisticated manner. Handling the astonishing revelation extremely well, the guests enter into a conversation with the cat, who exudes cool detachment. When Lady Blemley apologizes for spilling some of his milk, Tobermory merely replies: 'After all, it's not my Axminster.'[113] The atmosphere turns from astonishment to deep concern when it transpires that Tobermory does not shy away from speaking the truth, slowly but surely exposing the hidden secrets and failings of Lady Blemley's guests. In response to Mavis Pellington's questions regarding his opinion on human intelligence, he happily elaborates:

> When your inclusion in this house-party was suggested Sir Wilfrid protested that you were the most brainless woman of his acquaintance, and that there was a wide distinction between hospitality and the care of the feeble-minded…[114]

And so he continues.

The ability of cats to hide away in nooks and crannies, to be silent observers of human drama, has obviously enabled

Tobermory to see and hear things that the individuals in question would rather have remained hidden. His new-found talent causes the party much anxiety – they wonder if he could teach other cats to talk and spread their shameful secrets to a wider circle. The tables are very much turned – the pet has become the master. Unfortunately for Tobermory, but luckily for the humans in this story, he comes to a sticky end and any scandal is narrowly avoided.

Tobermory certainly is an unusual creature, but not as unusual as the character of Monsieur Tibault in Stephen Vincent Benét's story 'The King of the Cats'. We meet a group of New York high-society members who are fizzing with excitement as they await the arrival of the famed conductor M. Tibault for a series of concerts. But what makes the prospect of seeing him in the flesh even more exciting is the fact that he sports what can only be described as a – tail. We first encounter the conductor as he walks on stage for the first highly anticipated concert:

> he did not walk on, he strolled, leisurely, easily, aloofly, the famous tail curled nonchalantly about one wrist – a suave, black panther lounging through a summer garden.[115]

A member of the group, Tommy Brooks, is less enthusiastic as his love interest, the beautiful, mysterious Princess Vivrakanarda, seems to share a deep, inexplicable connection with M. Tibault. Both of them appear to have a feline quality in their looks, their behaviour and their movements, which sets them apart from other people. Tommy becomes more and more agitated, especially as he one day notices that M. Tibault appears to be hiding the fact that his legs are covered in black fur. He is now convinced that this is no man, but a cat. Together with his aptly named friend Billy Strange, he concocts a plan to discover M. Tibault's true identity, spurred on by the fact that the princess and Tibault become engaged. Their plan is inspired by a folklore tale, *The King of the Cats*, known and retold across the British Isles for centuries (this is, in fact, true – even the poet Shelley took note of this tale in his diary). The story exists in several slightly different versions, but usually involves a man witnessing a funeral held by cats. He then shares his extraordinary experience with a friend, at which point a house cat resting nearby usually leaps up and exclaims that the king of cats is dead and he will now be reigning over the felines.

Tommy proceeds to share a version of this story at a dinner party attended by Tibault and the princess, pretending all the while it was he who saw this cat funeral. And, to Tommy's surprise, Tibault suddenly exclaims 'Then I'm the King of the Cats!'[116] and vanishes in a flash of light and smoke. The princess does not marry Tommy, but instead escapes America with a seemingly broken heart.

Similarly to Kipling's 'The Cat that Walked by Himself', Patricia Highsmith's short story 'Ming's Biggest Prey' also ponders a close relationship between a woman and her cat, contrasting it with the male attitude towards the feline companion. The story is told from Ming's perspective, not in the first but in the third person, which allows the reader to see the world through the eyes of the cat whilst also maintaining the otherness of the feline viewpoint. Highsmith's writing conveys in vibrant detail the world as experienced through feline senses, enabling the reader to almost taste the delight of a delicious bit of lobster and feel the warmth of the sun on soft fur. She also explores Ming's thoughts on humans in some detail – the fact that Ming generally does not like people, as they mostly do not consider his feelings or needs. The only exception to this is Elaine, whom he belongs to: 'In all the world, he liked only Elaine.'[117]

Unfortunately, their harmonious set-up is now being disturbed by Teddie, Elaine's love interest. Teddie does not like Ming, and Ming hates Teddie. It quickly transpires that the cat's animosity is justified as Teddie not only tries to kill Ming but is also stealing from Elaine. As the situation escalates, Ming manages to escape the murder attempt, due to his natural feline abilities, and his counter-attack surprisingly results in Teddie falling to his death. The death seems accidental, as Ming reacts instinctively and in defence. But it certainly is the outcome which Ming desires most – being left alone with his favourite human, Elaine, and relishing the love and attention she lavishes on him.

CAT NARRATORS

'I am a cat.'[118] With those four words it could be argued that feline fiction has its 'Call me Ishmael' moment. A short, iconic opening line that, simply and directly, identifies its narrator and sets the tone for the story that follows. The novel in question is actually entitled *I Am a Cat* and was written by the Japanese writer Natsume Sōseki. It was published as a serial in the literary journal *Hototogisu* during 1905 and 1906, was hugely popular at the time, has gone on to become a classic of Japanese, and global, literature and can claim significant cultural impact beyond the world of books.

The novel is narrated by an unnamed cat who cannot remember when or where he was born. He has been wandering the streets for some time, suffering cruelty at the hands of humans, when he is taken in by a schoolteacher and his family, despite the protestations of their housekeeper, from whom the cat has stolen a fish. Through feline eyes we watch the comings and goings, the secrets and aspirations of the household, and their regular visitors and guests. *I Am a Cat* is a satire on Japanese middle-class society during the Meiji period, and particularly the way Western culture and values were starting to be subsumed into that society. At one point, influenced by the work of an Italian artist, the teacher attempts to draw the cat in a realistic style. The cat, trying to be helpful, stays put for as long as possible, even though 'there is no conceivable resemblance between myself and that queer thing which my master is creating'. He then goes on to critique the artwork in detail, and the whole of the book is essentially a cat observing and critiquing human life. He does not think highly of our species and is convinced that the human race will soon fail, leaving cats to take over.

The cat narrates the book in a style that would have been considered archaic even in the early 1900s, his voice in Japanese coming across as that of some ancient aristocrat, and this creates a slightly pompous tone that elevates the comedy in the original language. Most English translations are unable to convey that in quite the same way, but you still get a sense of the cat's elevated opinion of himself. One legacy of this style is Sōseki's use of the personal pronoun *wagahai* in the cat's narration. While almost never spoken in general Japanese language today, it remains in use in fiction for anthropomorphized animals, especially those with a pompous or arrogant attitude. Sōseki's cat's influence can even be seen in modern technology, with the Mario character Bowser, the turtle king bad guy, using the archaic word *wagahai* in his many computer-game appearances from Super Mario Bros to Mario Kart and beyond.

If you've ever observed a cat and wondered what it makes of the fact that it has a tail, then the narrator of 'The Tail', a 1988 short story by M.J. Engh, may have some answers for you. Angered by some particularly frustrating birds on the other side of a window, it lashes its tail a few times to relieve its rage, only for the tail to give one extra spasm of its own.

> I do not think you can understand. Perhaps if your right hand suddenly struck you in the face you would feel something of what I felt. But a hand cannot compare with a tail. At all times, a tail has its own character. It is not a part, like a hand or paw; it is a whole.[119]

The cat spends some time teasing and playing with its tail, much to the amusement of nearby humans – 'I became aware that they were laughing at me' – and then he offers an opinion that may well be shared by many cats: 'One does not expect much understanding from humans, but one all too easily grows fond of them.'

He leaves the room, a little humiliated, and beats his tail into submission before licking it affectionately, with one last reminder to the reader that when we see a cat playing with its tail we cannot truly understand what is going on. It is a fine example of an author getting into the psyche of a cat and sharing its thoughts on the page, and convincingly so.

In American novelist Charles Baxter's 2020 novel *The Sun Collective* Harold and Alma Brettigan are a retired couple trying to cope with the fact that their adult son, an actor, has vanished, seemingly preferring a life on the streets to the comfort of the family home. In their search for him, they become involved with the Sun Collective of the title, an altruistic organization that helps the homeless but that slowly reveals itself to be more of a cult, and one that possibly harbours terrorist aims.

Early on in the novel, Alma suffers a stroke-like episode, after which she is convinced she has the ability to converse with her pet dog and cat, much to the concern and eventual annoyance of her husband. And, as she relays the conversations to Harold, the animals display personalities that most pet owners will recognize. The dog is friendly and eager to please, whereas the cat distrusts almost everyone, and shares its opinions on any visitors who come to the home. In a delightful nod to *The Master and Margarita*, the animals are named Woland and Behemoth.

We have enjoyed cats that talk to human characters within the novels they inhabit, as well as cats that narrate stories and, in a way, are talking directly to readers, but, as teased at the beginning of this chapter, there is at least one book that has actually been written by a cat, and it has proved so popular that it has been translated into many languages and is still in print 200 years later. The feline 'author' is Tomcat Murr and the book he 'wrote' is, to give it its full title, *The Life and Opinions of the Tomcat Murr together with a fragmentary Biography of Kapellmeister Johannes Kreisler on Random Sheets of Waste Paper.*

The premiss of *Tomcat Murr* is a delightful conceit. The autodidact Murr has taught himself to read and write and has composed his memoirs, using pages from a book about a musician named Johannes Kreisler as blotting paper. But when the cat's manuscript goes to print, both texts are included by accident, so the story now alternates between Murr's memoir and Kreisler's biography, the changes often coming mid-sentence. It takes a while for the reader to get used to this device, and to balance both narratives, but once the format settles into a pattern two highly enjoyable stories emerge, stories that complement, mirror and engage with each other in subtle and intricate ways.

Murr's human owner is a man known as Master Abraham, and Abraham also happens to be mentor to Kreisler, so his presence links the two texts. Murr appears early on in Kreisler's biography, and the cat mentions the musician within his memoir, but there are many other references and events that echo between the fragments the reader is presented with. Murr himself is a bit of a show-off and never misses an opportunity to allude to his education by mention-ing books he has read and music he likes to listen to – Mozart and Shakespeare are name-dropped, for example – and some of these cross over neatly into the alternate text. It is hard not to be impressed by the complexity and the way in which this book from two centuries ago is more experimental and inventive than much contemporary literature.

Of course, *Tomcat Murr* is not actually written by a cat, and Johannes Kreisler never composed or played a note of music. Both characters are inventions of E.T.A. Hoffman, who was born in Königsberg in 1776 and came to writing in his thirties. This was his second and final novel. It was published in two volumes, the first at Christmas 1819 and the second two years later – there was meant to be a third but Hoffman died in 1822 leaving it unfinished. Although Murr and Kreisler are fictional, they do have real-life counterparts. Hoffman himself was a composer before he became an author, with several operas to his name. Such was his love of music, and Mozart in particular, that he changed his name from Ernst Theodore *Wilhelm* Hoffmann to Ernst Theodore *Amadeus* Hoffmann. Many of the works attributed to Kreisler in the book are clearly based on the author's own compositions. And Hoffmann owned a much-beloved tabby cat named Murr, who was two years old when he began writing the novel.

We know that Hoffmann was a fan of *The Life and Opinions of Tristram Shandy* by Laurence Sterne – Anthea Bell's splendid modern translation of *Tomcat Murr* deliberately references Shandy's title – and some of his very earliest writing played around with Sterne's experimental visual techniques, but *Tomcat Murr* was itself a big influence on writers that were to follow. Thomas Mann's novel *Doctor Faustus* has clear parallels, especially with the fictional composer at the centre of its plot; Behemoth, the cat in *The Master and Margarita*, a novel we discuss elsewhere in this book, owes a huge debt to Murr; readers of David Mitchell's best-selling

Cloud Atlas will have spotted similarities with the concept of narratives breaking off mid-sentence; and German author Christa Wolf even wrote a sequel, of sorts, in the 1970s.

Most of the books this chapter have examined, in one way or another, the way cats relate to and communicate with humans, and vice versa. A fascinating aspect of Nilanjana Roy's novel *The Wildings* is her exploration of the way cats communicate with each other.

We find ourselves in one of Delhi's oldest neighbourhoods, an area full of wild and feral cats that roam the streets freely and fend for themselves within the hustle and bustle of the busy city. There are gangs and leaders, hierarchies and histories, and a network of communication that is based on a sort of localized telepathy. Cats can communicate with each other through their thoughts, sometimes over long distances, through a method known as 'linking'. It is a system that works, that builds friendships and allegiances as well as cementing rivalries and feuds, but it is limited to their own species and can convey only so much information.

But into this established order comes a new voice, a confused and vague new voice but one which can broadcast to all cats far and wide, can convey emotion as well as information, and, most importantly, can communicate with any species. It is a Sender, a special cat that comes once in a generation, and one that threatens to overthrow the natural order of things. When the wild cats of Delhi realize that the

Sender is not only a kitten but also a pampered house cat, they decide that the best thing to do is track it down and kill it.

The Wildings was published as a novel for young adults, but, as the endorsement from Salman Rushdie on the cover suggests, it has a broader appeal than that. It is a feline *Watership Down*; like that classic it is prepared to go to some very dark places, and – also like Richard Adams's novel – it is a book that readers of any age can appreciate. The sequel, *The Hundred Names of Darkness*, sees the Delhi cats battling against dogs, snakes and, worst of all, humans.

As we have seen, whether a story has a feline narrator, or features a speaking cat within its pages, or even claims to have been written by a cat, certain traits crop up time and time again – a degree of aloofness, the opinion that cat and human are equals, a selfish 'what can I get out of this?' attitude, and many others that readers will recognize in the cats that live in their homes. Writers have, many times, tried to capture the feline voice; it is fascinating to see not only the many different ways in which they have done so, but also the numerous similarities.

AUTHORS *and their* CATS

W RITING IS, BY AND LARGE, A SOLITARY PURSUIT, and one that is not always conducive to maintaining healthy relationships – at least, not with fellow human beings. The literary world is full of doomed love affairs and fractured friendships, both on and off the page – from Gatsby and Daisy to the real-life travails of Virginia Woolf and Vita Sackville-West, from the slow estrangement of Sebastian Flyte and Charles Ryder to the bitter feud between Paul Theroux and V.S. Naipaul. And while failed romances may create the inspiration for, and the plots of, great novels, they rarely deliver a happy ending. Perhaps this is why many authors turn to companions who will tolerate their antisocial lifestyles, the hours spent at the desk, and the mood swings – from frustration at a problematic plot point to the joy following a well-crafted sentence. Such a companion is often a cat.

The list of authors who have shared their lives with cats is seemingly endless. Alexandre Dumas grew up with a family cat named Mysouff, who would walk with him to the corner when he set off for work in the morning and would be waiting on the same corner when he arrived home in the evening. As an older man he owned a cat he called Mysouff II in tribute. Mark Twain once said that, 'When a man loves cats, I am his friend and comrade, without further introduction.' Following the death of his wife, Twain's constant companion was Bambino, who ran off to chase a squirrel one day and did not come back. Twain placed ads in all the local newspapers, and kind strangers would turn up with found strays, but his beloved pet was never seen again.

Felines also star in some of his fiction: in the short story 'Dick Baker's Cat', a cat called Tom Quartz seems to have a sixth sense of where to find gold. His owner, Dick, talks affectionately of the seemingly supernatural abilities of his companion, admiring his intelligence and dignity. Unfortunately, when Dick and his partner turn to quartz mining, which involves the occasional explosion in the mining shaft, Tom is far from happy. He accidentally becomes the victim of one of these explosions, barely surviving the blast. After that, the cat displays nothing but disgust for quartz mining. The story speaks of Twain's affection for the headstrong feline character, assigning them wisdom far beyond human reach.

Even a famous recluse such as J.D. Salinger, author of *The Catcher in the Rye*, was apparently fond of cats. A collection of letters, postcards and photographs sent to his friend Donald Hartog include an image of Salinger and his Russian Blues and mention his cats several times, as well as ponder why he ever liked dogs.

At one point in the late 1950s, Ray Bradbury's house was home to twenty-two felines; his favourite was one that acted as a paperweight for his manuscripts. Gillian Flynn, author of *Gone Girl*, has always kept a black cat as a pet. Haruki Murakami owned a jazz club as a young man and named it Peter Cat, in honour of the cat he and his wife Yoko had at home. Sylvia Plath's childhood cat was named Daddy. Edward Gorey was said to like cats more than people. Samuel Johnson refused to let his servants buy food for his cat, Hodge, and would go out and fetch oysters for him. Jean Cocteau reportedly developed his love of cats after living next door to Colette for many years, and he even went on to become president of the Cats Friends' Club in Paris, a feline appreciation society. When asked why he liked cats so much he replied, 'I prefer cats over dogs because police cats don't exist.'

CRITICAL CATS

Why do cats play such an important role in the lives of so many writers? Ernest Hemingway confidently declared that the 'cat has absolute emotional honesty. Human beings, for one reason or another, may hide their feelings, but a cat does not.' Not everyone will agree with his faith in the animal's inability to deceive, but he hints at an intriguing way of interpreting the cat–writer relationship. Perhaps, in a world where the writer's work is judged and reviewed by his readers and critics, cats are the honest companion; the creature which does not pretend or ingratiate itself. Usefully, neither do they speak, so their silent aura dispels loneliness in the solitary act of writing, without interrupting the process. Hemingway kept many cats, fondly referring to them as 'purr factories' and 'love sponges'. He was once given a six-toed cat by a ship's captain, which he christened Snow White. To this day, descendants of Snow White, each with an extra toe, live at Hemingway's former home in Florida, now a museum dedicated to the author. In his short story 'Cat in the Rain', a woman watches the world go by from her hotel balcony and notices a cat in the rain. She insists on rescuing the poor animal, whilst her husband shows little interest. By the time she has made it outdoors, the cat is gone, but the episode triggers a sudden wish to change her life – to create a home, change her look to be more feminine and to own a cat: 'I want a cat. I want a cat now.'[120] The cat represents her craving to settle down, to have someone to care for and love. What would be more perfect than a 'love sponge'?

Nobel laureate Doris Lessing grew up in rural Africa surrounded by animals, among them a large number of cats. These were not the well-groomed pets we might be familiar with now, but half-feral creatures, living in the great outdoors. In *Particularly Cats*, she describes dark memories from her childhood, seeing her parents forced to kill many of the cats roaming her family's land as their numbers regularly rocketed. The contrast between the farm cats and the cats she shared her home with later in life could not be starker – the latter recognized as individual characters rather than a mass of anonymous animals.

She ponders the human–feline interdependency in a series of books devoted to cats, including *Particularly Cats* and *On Cats*, describing her conflicting feelings over whether humans should turn wild animals into domesticated creatures, whether it is right for humans to interfere with nature and claim ownership of animals. Lessing demonstrates a deep appreciation and fondness for cats, relishing their individual characters and the impact they have had on her life. Her cat El Magnifico, or Butchkin, immortalized in her novella *The Old Age of El Magnifico*, was a constant companion during much of her writing life. When he grew ill, she was tormented by her inability to speak to him, to ask him whether he was in pain, what treatment he would wish to receive. Rather than simply enjoying their company, though, we can see that Lessing is provoked to consider deeper issues by the presence of these animals in her life – issues relating to humanity and nature, and even the complexities of motherhood.

The fact that many writers have chosen cats as pets, and formed long-lasting bonds with them, is not surprising in itself, but some of the greatest feline enthusiasts may surprise you. The founders of the Beat Generation were notorious for their appetite for psychedelic drugs and sexual liberation, as well as their rejection of materialism and traditional narrative structure, but what is perhaps less well known is their shared love of cats. In a 1954 letter to Jack Kerouac, Allen Ginsberg commented that 'a cat sits on my shoulder as I write this'.[121] Which cat he was referring to is unclear, but he owned a number during his life, including the period he spent in a rundown room at the 'Beat Hotel' in Paris with many of his fellow writers.

It was there, in 1958, that William Burroughs completed the text of his most famous novel, *Naked Lunch*, although it was nearly thirty years later that he wrote *The Cat Inside*, a novella-cum-memoir in which he reminisces about his many feline companions, including the splendidly named Calico Jane (named in honour of Jane Bowles), Rooski and Wimpy. Rooski was a particular favourite, with a distraught Burroughs frantically contacting city authorities when the cat went missing one day. The author knew his cat was in trouble, sensing a Mayday signal in the air. The lost cat was discovered in the pound, hours away from a 'humane death' – Burroughs only securing his release upon payment of a fine and agreeing to rabies injections. *The Cat Inside* also captures Burroughs's take on the feline nature: 'The cat does not offer services. The cat offers itself. You don't buy love for nothing. Like all pure creatures, cats are practical.'[122] Poet Charles Bukowski also adored cats, almost as much as he seemingly hated people, and wrote several poems about his pets, including 'The History of One Tough Motherfucker' about his white tailless cat Manx.

In *Big Sur*, a largely autobiographical novel, Jack Kerouac writes movingly about the death of his favourite cat, Tyke. Kerouac felt a particular emotional connection with cats because they reminded him of his late brother, Gerard. As toddlers, the two boys would lie on their bellies and watch the family cats lap up milk. Gerard died of rheumatic fever at the age of 9, a loss that plagued Jack for the rest of his life. The loss of Tyke also hit him hard, if the eulogy in *Big Sur* is anything to go by: 'It was exactly and no lie and sincerely like the death of my little brother – I loved Tyke with all my heart, he was my baby who as a kitten just slept in the palm of my hand and with his little head hanging down.'[123]

It is perhaps unsurprising that the death of a beloved family pet can inspire writers to put pen to paper, but this may not always be in the form of moving tribute. As we learnt in a previous chapter, Stephen King wrote what many readers consider his darkest novel, *Pet Sematary*, after his daughter's cat, Smucky, was run over by a car on Thanksgiving. The cat's small wooden cross carried the words 'Smucky – he was obedient', but, as King pointed out in a 2019 interview, 'I mean, he was a cat. He wasn't f—ing obedient!'

It is often said that dogs resemble their owners, but is the same true for cats? Or, perhaps more pertinent to this chapter, can authors grow to resemble their feline companions? Colette, whose poignant short story 'The Cat' we encounter in our 'Cats in Translation' chapter, was fond of animals, spending her life surrounded by a number of dogs and cats. She published three volumes, entitled *Dialogues de bêtes*, containing imagined conversations between her French bulldog Toby-Dog and Maltese cat Kiki-the-Demure. The *London Review of Books* went so far as to refer to her as 'the frizzle-headed Cat Woman of 20th-century French writing', possibly because of her ability to lend her writing a feline tone of sensuality and detachment in equal measure. Much like Hemingway, Colette believed that animals were incapable of deceit, their actions determined by natural instinct, which elevated them above fallible humans. She clearly admired cats and felt kinship with them – so much so that her friends and acquaintances regularly commented on a certain feline quality she possessed. Colette happily cultivated this comparison by dressing up for the dance-hall stage as a seductive wildcat.

It might seem counter-intuitive to picture the master of Gothic horror Edgar Allan Poe, creator of such masterpieces as 'The Masque of the Red Death' and 'The Raven', in a cosy scene with a purring cat. Especially if we consider that one of his most acclaimed short stories, 'The Black Cat', which we discussed earlier in the book, contains the torture and murder of the cat itself. Why, then, are we counting Poe among literary cat lovers? If we look beyond his fictional works, his essays and letters give a glimpse of the role cats played in Poe's life. An introduction to an edition of his complete collection of essays describes the passing of Poe's young wife, after much suffering and long illness.

> A friend of the family pictures the death-bed scene – mother and husband trying to impart warmth to her by chafing her hands and her feet, while her pet cat was suffered to nestle upon her bosom for the sake of added warmth.[124]

The cat is not merely a pet, but a family member, given access and indeed an active role in this intimate and heart-breaking moment.

Throughout his life, Poe struggled with depression and alcoholism, in addition to his wife's illness and a constant lack of money. Some claim that the writer became dis-illusioned with humanity and expected little in the way of support from his contemporaries. In contrast, when writing about his tortoiseshell cat, Catterina, he was often full of enthusiasm and warmth, such as in a letter to his mother-in-law: 'Sissy had a hearty cry last night, because you and Catterina weren't there... Give our best love to Catterina.'[125]

It seems that he not only valued the emotional comfort provided by cats, but also admired their natural instincts. He observed one of his cats cunningly open the kitchen door, leading him to speculate in his essay 'Instinct vs. Reason – A Black Cat' that the creature has much more sophisticated intellectual abilities than we usually give it credit for. He certainly enjoyed their company, if reports that he permitted Catterina to be present during his readings are to be believed. Catterina is even said to have sat on Poe's shoulders when he was writing (a position Ginsberg's cat appears to have adopted more than a century later). It seems likely that, in a life marked by hardship, both physical and emotional, his pets provided some comfort and stability – Catterina living with the Poe family for thirteen years and, poignantly, passing away shortly after Poe's own death.

PREFERRED COMPANIONS

Is the presence of a feline companion really conducive to writing? The prolific Joyce Carol Oates, who has written well over a hundred books, certainly seems to think so, claiming, 'I write so much because my cat sits on my lap. She purrs so I don't want to get up. She's so much more calming than my husband.' And Oates is not the only author to acclaim the benefits of keeping a cat when you subscribe to the writing life. Ursula K. Le Guin (who wrote an auto-biography of her cat Pardner, which is titled *My Life So Far* and claims to be translated into English from the Feline) rated cats over canines, 'Maybe because writers don't want to have to stop writing and walk the dog.' Authors who are fond of procrastination may disagree.

Oates was a vociferous contributor to a rather unusual debate hosted by David Remnick, editor of the *New Yorker*, in 2014, about whether dogs or cats make for better compan-ions. Among the panellists were such luminaries as Malcolm Gladwell (pro-dog) and actor Jesse Eisenberg (sending a cat-supporting message all the way from Hawaii). Oates herself presented, with great flourish, 'Jubilate: An Homage in Caterell' – a poem about her cat Cherie and an ode to the cat's independent and mysterious nature, in which she references it as muse to many a writer, and as 'the harshest critic of prose'. She claims that the best literary works 'are not ghost- but cat-written'.[126] She values cats as companions to the creative mind, whilst also perceiving them as beings of a higher nature. Cats have been her constant companions, among them Reynard, and the aforementioned Cherie. Her love of cats has been expressed in an anthology, *The Sophisticated Cat*, as well as several children's books featuring cat characters (and which feature happier endings than her fiction for adults). Occasionally, she even goes so far as to tweet from the perspective of her cat.

Audrey Niffenegger, author of the bestselling *The Time Traveler's Wife*, has talked in interviews about the two cats that share her home. Cats also appear in some of her work. Her dark short story 'Secret Life with Cats' was allegedly inspired by her experience of working at a cat shelter; it features some scary cats who show their love for their favourite human Ruth in a rather unusual way, as they eat her corpse to bring her back after her death.

V.S. Naipaul's essay 'The Strangeness of Grief', on the other hand, turns to weightier subjects and is a moving contemplation of loss, exploring the passing of his father and brother, as well as of his beloved cat Augustus. Naipaul describes a journey of wonder and delight when Augustus comes into his life as a kitten, as he discovers the unique qualities and abilities of his new companion. But, as he states with a sense of foreboding, 'with cats, so brief is their span, every sign of vigor invariably comes with a foreshadowing of decay.'[127] As Augustus's health declines, we can sense Naipaul's distress at seeing the once graceful and independent animal lose his strength and experience great pain. When Augustus's suffering becomes unbearable and the vet has to put him down, Naipaul mourns the loss of this beautiful creature that gave him so much joy. He struggles to think of his body decaying in the ground but eventually finds comfort in the thought that Augustus might still be present somehow, observing and pondering only as cats can do.

BLACK CATS

Bohumil Hrabal was a giant of twentieth-century Czech literature and was revered by many of his contemporaries, including Milan Kundera and Philip Roth. He is best known in the English-speaking world for his 1964 novel *Closely Observed Trains*, which was adapted into an Oscar-winning film, and he happened to be another literary cat lover, although one with more of a tragic element than many.

In the late 1980s he wrote *All My Cats*, a memoir of his life with his cats. It is one of the most traumatic books we have come across in this compendium. It starts out sweetly enough, with Hrabal making frequent trips from his apartment in Prague to his small country cottage in Kersko, a journey of about an hour by bus. There he is greeted by five cats that he and his wife have accidentally adopted – although Mrs Hrabal's frequent cries of 'What are we going to do with all these cats?' suggests she wasn't quite as keen on them as he was – and who rush in through the back door as soon as it is opened. Bohumil adores these cats, greeting them one by one in turn, although his favourite is an older female cat named Blackie:

I never tired of looking at her and she was so fond of me
she'd practically swoon whenever I picked her up and
held her to my forehead and whispered sweet words in her
ear.[128]

He paints a vivid and amusing picture of the mild chaos
of five cats in the same house, especially of *meshugge Stunde*,
or the 'crazy hour' that most cat owners will recognize, that
period in every day when furry bodies fly around the room
chasing each other, or any remotely mobile inanimate object.
But at some point in every visit there comes a time to return
to the city and the five cats will poke their heads through
the garden fence, with pleading looks that make Hrabal feel
guilty for the entire journey home. It is never explained
quite how the cats are looked after while he is away, but the
implication is that they fend for themselves, killing the local
wildlife when they are in need of a decent meal.

The book progresses with more back and forth from
city to countryside, and various feline anecdotes, until two
of the cats fall pregnant. Hrabal is initially delighted but
then realizes that he will probably have to get rid of some
of the kittens, and his underlying guilt keeps building and
building until the fateful day arrives. What follows is a quite
harrowing murder scene that will go on to haunt Hrabal,
and would probably haunt the reader too so we won't go
into more detail here, except to say that the whole process is
repeated a year later with two more pregnancies.

Hrabal was clearly a man with a deep love of cats, and saw them as wonderful companions, especially for a writer, but he was also prepared to take action to keep the feline population at a manageable level, even if his brutal actions caused him deep psychological anguish, at times to the point of contemplating his own death. We must remember that all of this took place in Communist Czechoslovakia many decades ago, when the more humane practice of neutering cats was not really an option, but that won't stop the reader from flinching at some of the scenes contained in the book.

As a sad postscript, Bohumil Hrabal himself died in 1997, at the age of 82, after falling from a hospital window while trying to feed the pigeons. His doctor considered it to be suicide.

We can see that cats have often managed to work their way onto the shoulders, and laps, of great authors, but some have gone one step further and made it onto the pages their owners have written. Neil Gaiman regularly blogs about his cats. His short story 'The Price' was inspired by a stray black cat that he and his family adopted. Here Gaiman celebrates a cat's loyalty to his human family, its fierce determination to protect them from harm, even if it is the Devil himself that he has to face. The narrator asks, 'I wonder what we did to deserve the Black Cat',[129] hinting at the great impact a cat can have on our lives. But none can perhaps surpass Raymond

Chandler's cat, who, not satisfied with being written about, decided to take up writing herself. At least that is what the evidence suggests, given the number of surviving letters to correspondents penned by Chandler's 'secretary', Taki.

Finally, special mention in this chapter is given to Spider, a black cat, possibly part-Siamese, with enormous green eyes, who was owned by not one but two world-renowned authors. He initially belonged to, and was much loved by, Patricia Highsmith. She dedicated her 1964 crime novel *The Glass Cell* to him:

> To my dear cat
> SPIDER
> born in Palisades, New York,
> now a resident of Positano,
> my cellmate for most of these pages.

When Highsmith moved from Positano, Italy, to live in Surrey in England, she was unable to take Spider with her and arranged to leave him with friends, but that didn't work out and the cat ended up with Muriel Spark, who was living in Rome. 'It was supposed to be a temporary arrangement,' Spark told Highsmith's biographer, Joan Schenkar, 'but after I got to know him I couldn't let him go.' Spark and Highsmith never met, the fostering having been set up via mutual friends, but the two corresponded for some years, mainly about Spider. Both were devastated when he died, Spark later commenting: 'You could tell he had been a writer's cat. He would sit by me, seriously, as I wrote, while all my other cats filtered away.'[130]

The evidence does seem to suggest that cats make ideal pets for writers, whether it be the simple fact that they are content to curl up on a lap while, above them, their owner taps away at a keyboard, or for more complex psychological reasons. There is certainly no shortage of literary greats who have been happy to record the existence, and influence, of their feline friends, guaranteeing that they will never be forgotten. And even a cursory glance at the social media feeds of the popular authors of today will reveal numerous photos of cats sprawled across desks admiring their owner's work – or occasionally interrupting it – suggesting that the role of cats behind the scenes in literature is not going to diminish any time soon.

ASTROCATS

I T COULD BE ARGUED, AND INDEED WE ARE ARGUING IT here, that no animal, apart from humans, appears in the many and varied works of science fiction as much as the cat. We can only offer anecdotal evidence for this – we have read a lot of books during our research – but there is also a core logic to our claim.

For more than 2,000 years, when people took to the seas they have taken feline companions with them. The idea of the ship's cat will be familiar to everyone – a four-legged crew member employed to keep the decks clear of mice and rats. As we saw in the introduction, archaeological evidence suggests that Ancient Egyptian cats spread along Mediterranean trading routes from the eighth century BCE, reaching as far as a Viking port in the Baltic Sea.

It is likely that every major voyage of the Age of Discovery, such as those of Vasco da Gama, Christopher Columbus and Ferdinand Magellan, featured a cat or two among the crew. Ship's cats have been around for a very long time.

It makes some sense, therefore, that when the authors of speculative fiction created stories set on *space*ships, they chose to continue this tradition by including cats among the crew. The novels and short stories of science fiction are full of feline space travellers.

CATS ON BOARD

The Barque Cats are descended from Tuxedo Thomas, a Maine Coon cat that was one of the first interstellar companions for humans in space. In a series of books by Anne McCaffrey and Elizabeth Ann Scarborough, Thomas's progeny are highly prized crew members, responsible for keeping spacecraft free from vermin, but also for the morale boost they give to the humans they work alongside. Of course, this being science fiction, there is a little more to them than that, and as the series progresses the cats develop telepathy, a skill that makes them even more sought after, and embroils them in a plot to take over the universe.

Intergalactic domination is not remotely on the mind of Tommy, the space-station cat that features in 'Who's

There?', a short story by Arthur C. Clarke. When the station supervisor is asked to perform a space walk in order to clear some satellite debris, he dons his suit, which is 'completely different from flexible affairs men wear when they want to walk around on the moon'. Instead it is a 7-foot-long cylinder with internal controls, more like a mini spaceship than an outfit. Fuel, oxygen and battery readings all look good, but once he is floating through space the supervisor senses that something is wrong, seriously wrong. The noises in his suit are not normal, and he can feel a pressure on his neck; he starts to panic and smacks his head on the control panel, knocking himself unconscious. He comes to an hour later in the medical bay, but the doctors are 'much too busy playing with the three cute little kittens our badly misnamed Tommy had been rearing in the seclusion of my spacesuit's Number Five Storage Locker'.[131]

Cats on spaceships have even been the subject of poetry. In 'Tales of a Starship's Cat' by Judith R. Conly, the cat in question wanders the 'sleep-quiet' corridors and 'ladders ill-designed for feline feet' to the engine room, where it finds comfort in the 'great maternal purr'[132] of the machines.

A ship's cat is a traditional mascot of good luck on every vessel of the I.A.T.A (Intergalactic Assay and Trade Association) fleet. Therefore, in 'Well Worth the Money' by Jody Lynn Nye, Kelvin is welcomed aboard *Pandora*, a newly refitted vessel, by Balin Jurgenevski and his crew. The I.A.T.A. has negotiated with the blob-like Drebs that the aliens can pay for a trade debt by sharing their advanced technology, and Balin's mission is to test the first ship to be enhanced in this way. One of its features is an empathetic computer that can read the minds and satisfy the needs of the crew once they submit to its personality reader. This initially manifests itself with coffee served just the way they like it, and various in-flight entertainments, but it also extends to managing all aspects of the flight. The crew get so bored that they decide to submit Kelvin to the personality reader for a bit of fun. The computer, for all its state-of-the-art features, is incapable of discerning that Kelvin is 'just' a cat, and adds him to the payroll for the company as a pest controller. Soon it is responding to his every need, including feeding him some gourmet food the crew had brought on board for themselves, and giving him mice-related computer games to play with.

Kelvin comes into his own, in spectacular fashion, when *Pandora* is attacked by enemy aliens. The humans on board are paralysed by a weapon that alters their brain functions, but the cat is unaffected. He is scared and angry but he can still move. And that is when the ship responds to his needs and creates a more realistic computer game for him, using the ship's actual weapons. Kelvin is then battling the alien ship just as he did the digitized mice earlier. This ship's cat really does save the day and returns a hero, receiving a well-deserved bonus salary.

Cats go one stage further and pilot their own ships to fight alongside humans in 'The Game of Rat and Dragon', a landmark short story by Cordwainer Smith. Human telepaths are used to defend spaceships from Earth that are under attack from an invisible enemy. Regular humans cannot see these monsters, but the telepaths can perceive them as dragons. However, they need help in their quest to destroy them. This is where the cats come in. Cats can also perceive the enemy, but they see them as rats. Each telepath teams up with a feline companion and together they battle the dragon/rats by shooting at them with pinlights, tiny nuclear weapons. This may sound a little ridiculous but somehow Smith pulls it off, perhaps because he focuses on the relationship between one human telepath, Underhill, and his feline partner, Lady May. Following them into battle, and on to its aftermath, the reader can appreciate the bond between them and, no matter how literally out of this world their situation, compare it to the more domestic bond between humans and cats in real life. Lady May is rightly one of the most revered feline characters in science fiction.

Cordwainer Smith is one of many pseudonyms of the American writer Paul Linebarger, whose remarkable, if relatively short, life was reflected in his equally remarkable writing. Linebarger's father was involved in East Asian politics in the early years of the twentieth century. He sent his wife, pregnant with Paul, back to the USA from China to give birth so that their son would be eligible to run for president. This was a rather ambitious long-term aim and – spoiler alert in case you aren't up to speed on American presidents – did not come to pass. However, Linebarger Jr did become involved in politics. He was considered an expert on East Asia, writing several books on the subject, which was surely prompted by his father, and perhaps helped a little by the fact that his godfather was none other than Sun Yat-sen, the first president of the Republic of China. Paul also acted as an adviser to JFK, so at least he got close to the top job, even if he didn't achieve it himself. Somehow, Linebarger also found the time to write (using the Cordwainer Smith pen name) some of the most acclaimed science-fiction short stories and novellas of the 1950s and 1960s, a number of which are set in a fictional future version of Earth that is under the control of the Instrumentality of Mankind.

CAT MUTATIONS

Political allegories can be detected in 'The Ballad of Lost C'Mell', another of Smith's stories, in which humans live alongside hybrid animals, known as the Underpeople. These crossbreeds are treated like slaves and take on much of the menial work, a situation that has been the norm for many years. But Jestocost, one of the Lords of the Instrumentality, wants to help the Underpeople fight back and secure their freedom. He teams up with a catwoman named C'Mell and they instigate what amounts to a piece of telepathic hacking which, ultimately, allows the Underpeople to claim their freedom. The story joins a long list of science fiction that explores cat mutations, gets them walking on their hind legs, or features some form of feline alien race.

The Hani are maned and bearded creatures from the planet Anuurn, with a social hierarchy a bit like Earth lions. The adult males act as solitary lords over a clan of females and offspring; when the younger males are old enough to pose a threat, they are kicked out to fend for themselves, honing their battle skills until they are fit enough to take over a clan of their own. This behaviour means they are considered emotionally unstable, so when the Hani are gifted the technology required for interstellar travel by the primate-like Mahendo'sat race it is the females of the species that venture into space, leaving the men behind.

The political and trade alliances, and disagreements, of the Hani, Mahendo'sat and a range of other aliens with features similar to Earth creatures – including bipedal rat creatures called Kif; Stsho, a race that looks like crested birds; and the T'ca snake aliens – are the subject of *The Chanur Saga*, a series of novels by C.J. Cherryh. The books are noted for the way they explore cultural and linguistic differences, and for the changes that exposure to different species prompts in the key characters. There are a fair few battles and skirmishes – and who doesn't like the occasional explosion and laser beam in sci-fi? – but the main focus is on character and relationships, both personal and political, and that adds a depth that has won the series legions of human fans. How popular it is with cat aliens is unclear.

Far more warlike are the Kzinti, a race of carnivorous feline humanoids from the planet Kzin. During the multi-volume *Man-Kzin* series of stories they fight many wars with Earth forces and, somewhat grimly, develop a taste for human flesh. They first appear in a 1966 story titled 'The Warriors' by Larry Niven. Niven didn't consider himself best qualified to write about warfare, being more interested in fiction that examines scientific concepts and theories, so wasn't keen to publish more Man-Kzin stories. A number of his writer friends, however, wanted to explore the potential of the world Niven had created and he gave them permission to do so. As a result, the Man-Kzin Wars have evolved into a shared universe spanning dozens of stories and numerous authors, including Poul Anderson, Hal Colebatch and Jessica Q. Fox. Niven pops back from time to time to co-write a story, but the Kzinti have taken on a life of their own.

Another space cat that likes to attack humans is the Coeurl, a large black feline that features in 'Black Destroyer', a story by A.E. van Vogt that appeared in *Astounding Science*

Fiction magazine in July 1939. That issue is considered to mark the beginning of the golden age of science fiction (it also included an early appearance in print of Isaac Asimov; Robert A. Heinlein's first ever published story appeared in the August edition).

Coeurl is the last survivor of an ancient race and is struggling to find a fresh source of food when, as luck would have it, a spaceship full of scientists arrives and the prospect of a tasty lunch improves. The cat approaches the new arrivals, displaying all the signs of just being a curious animal, and the scientists register that it uses radio waves to communicate. Although they cannot understand it, they recognize it as an intelligent being and invite it onto the ship. Coeurl resists the urge to attack and observes the comings and goings for a while until he spots one scientist exploring outside on his own. That man is later found ripped to shreds; when examined, he is found to have been drained of all the phosphorus in his body.

There is only one real suspect in the crime, but the phosphorus thing bothers the scientists. They keep the cat alive and present it with a bowl of phosphorus which it goes crazy for, almost killing the man who gives it to him in the process. Convinced that this alien beast intends to carry on with its phosphorus buffet, they trap it and discuss what to do next. Unfortunately for them Coeurl is able to control 'vibrations of every description',[133] escapes through the wall and begins stalking and killing the crew. The excitement builds as the survivors attempt to thwart their cunning foe.

If the notion of a sinister dark alien picking off the crew of a spaceship one by one seems familiar, then it might interest you to know that Van Vogt accepted a $50,000 out-of-court settlement from 20th Century Fox, the production company behind the film *Alien*, for the similarities between his story and the movie that was released forty years later.[134]

Less horror or sci-fi, and more camp fantasy, is *Lyrec*, a 1986 novel by Gregory Frost. The title character is an interdimensional traveller who escapes his world just before it is destroyed by the evil Miradomon, who happens to have taken Lyrec's lover, Elystroya, with him. Lyrec is chasing Miradomon across worlds and dimensions, on a quest to rescue Elystroya, and arrives in the kind of medieval land that crops up in many a fantasy novel – plenty of swords, soldiers on horseback, scuffles in inns after a few too many meads. What is different about this adventure, though, is that Lyrec has a comrade and companion, Borregad, who has suffered a malfunction with his *crex*, the device used to travel from one dimension to another and to take corporeal form upon arrival. This dodgy crex means that, unlike Lyrec, Borregad cannot manifest himself as a human in this new land. Instead, he takes the form of a black cat, and he isn't happy about this at all.

Lyrec and Borregad clearly have a long shared history, and their camaraderie is evident in almost every conversation and interaction they have; it just so happens that, in the particular episode we get to witness in the book, this ribald banter is between a man and a talking cat. A rather grumpy talking cat at that. His feline form doesn't stop him getting drunk, fighting with soldiers and attempting to rescue his friend from a variety of scrapes, even if he often lacks the height and strength to help.

Although *Lyrec* is a rather broad example of the fantasy side of science fiction, and it is unlikely to be considered a classic of the genre, it is often entertaining, particularly when Borregad appears. An example of a memorable feline character in a rather less memorable novel.

Steampunk is a subgenre of sci-fi that blends the aesthetics of nineteenth century steam-powered industrial technology with the more modern concepts of science fiction – retro-futuristic, if you will – and it is a genre that has its fair share of cats. One of the most popular is Slag, the psychotic, battle-scarred ship's cat on board the *Ketty Jay*, a pirate airship at the centre of a quartet of novels by Chris Wooding. Wooding gives Slag his own narrative arc across the books and even hands some chapters over to the cat to narrate.

The Cinder Spires series, by Jim Butcher, is set in a world in which humans live in spires, huge towers reaching up into the sky, because the planet surface is full of dangerous beasts and, frankly, no one wants to go down there. In the first book, *The Aeronaut's Windlass*, Gwendolyn, Bridget and Bridget's best friend Rowl are members of a spire defence force who are recruited to lead an investigation into possible infiltration by an enemy spire. Skirmishes, plots, betrayals and dangers ensue, some of them involving that steampunk staple, airships, and one particular plot point seeing Rowl leading a 200-strong army of cats, Rowl himself being a talking cat and prince of his tribe.

WALKING THROUGH WALLS

Of course, some of the cats in science fiction are humble house cats here on Earth. A small kitten stuck on a window ledge, in 'Ordeal in Space' by Robert A. Heinlein, forces a man named William Saunders to face his fears. Some years before, Saunders was an astronaut involved in an accident. While repairing an antenna he was knocked into space; although eventually rescued, he has had a fear of heights ever since. The poor kitty stuck on the ledge knows nothing of this and mews plaintively while Saunders debates whether to rescue it or not.

A cat on a windowsill plays a crucial role in 'Mouse', a 1949 story by Frederic Brown. Leading biologist Bill Wheeler is sitting with his Siamese cat, named Beautiful, watching the world go by from his New York apartment window when they spot an alien spaceship land in Central Park. The cat hisses, her fur standing on end; she is alarmed and disturbed. Bill is altogether more nonchalant as he tries to calm her down:

> 'Quiet, Beautiful. It's all right. It's only a spaceship from Mars, to conquer Earth. It isn't a mouse.'[135]

But it turns out that it sort of is. Crowds assemble, the armed forces move in, awnings and tents go up around the ship, and soon Bill receives a phone call: he's the nearest eminent biologist and the government needs his help. He is asked to examine the dead creature that has been found in the otherwise empty vessel, a creature that looks very much like a mouse, albeit an alien one with different genetic make-up. For a short while Bill is at the centre of one of the greatest moments in history, at one point standing next to the president himself, but once his work is done the hoo-ha dies down and very little news comes his way. Until, that is, strange things start to happen. World leaders are assassinated, an atomic bomb accidentally goes off in a desert testing ground, stock markets crash. Bill becomes convinced that something other than a dead mouse arrived on the spaceship, a being without form that inhabited another creature, from which it began its subtle attack on Earth. And that is when he remembers Beautiful acting strangely when the ship landed. 'Mouse' is one of those early sci-fi stories that would have made an excellent episode of *Twilight Zone*, a blend of the extraordinary and the domestic, the meeting of alien life and a pet cat.

The positive impact cats can have on humans is explored in the astonishing dystopian novel *The Wall* by the Austrian writer Marlen Haushofer, translated by Shaun Whiteside. The unnamed female narrator is spending a few days in a remote hunting lodge with her friends and their dog. When her friends do not return from a walk into the nearest town, she becomes worried and decides to head out to investigate further. On her way she suddenly encounters a transparent wall which is impenetrable and seemingly endless – 'something invisible, smooth and cool'.[136] The narrator realizes she has been cut off from the rest of the world – she does not know what happened or what the future may bring. She can see humans and animals on the other side, but they seem to have been petrified or frozen in time, seemingly not alive anymore. Although she has an admirable ability to think practically in this extraordinary situation, almost immediately starting to work out how to make provisions last, she is of course facing the emotional effects of extreme isolation and uncertainty. In this turmoil, the only living creatures to provide comfort and companionship are the animals who were trapped alongside the narrator in this restricted territory. Among these is a cat, which suddenly appears a few weeks after the wall came into existence.

Initially, the cat is suspicious of the narrator, who assumes that the animal has been treated badly by other people in the past. Slowly, but surely, the cat settles in and becomes part of the little community in the hunting lodge. As time goes on, the cat must have encountered a tom on her nocturnal expeditions into the woods, as she gives birth to several litters of kittens. The narrator cherishes having the cat and her offspring around; they bring her joy and comfort. Throughout, the cat maintains her feline independence, disappearing occasionally, which is reinforced by the fact that the narrator never gives her a name but simply refers to her as the cat. Recognizing the imbalance in their relationship, the narrator speculates: 'I don't think the cat needs me as desperately as I need her.'[137] Still, the cat and the kittens are part of the only family or community she has, and the affection she holds for these animals leave her vulnerable to grief when the kittens all disappear or die eventually, with only the cat matriarch left at the end.

As the name suggests, science fiction spends a lot of time exploring the fictional potential of science, and there is perhaps no more famous fictional cat in the world of science than Schrödinger's cat. This thought experiment, devised by physicist Erwin Schrödinger in 1935, posits that a hypothetical cat may be considered simultaneously both alive and dead as a result of its fate being linked to a random subatomic event that may or may not occur. This idea, originally born out of a discussion with Albert Einstein, resonates across many themes and plots in sci-fi novels and stories, but two stand out as being clearly linked to that original thought.

Ursula K. Le Guin offers an obvious tribute in the short story, 'Schrödinger's Cat', in which the narrator is informed by a visitor that the cat that had, until a few moments ago, been sitting on her lap is actually the real Schrödinger's cat, the former pet of the famous physicist. The visitor then insists that they recreate the thought experiment together; the narrator, after some initial hesitation, agrees. We won't spoil the ending of this story, but suffice to say all is not what it seems.

Pixel is the name of a cat that appears in two novels by Robert A. Heinlein, an author we have mentioned already in this chapter: *The Cat Who Walks through Walls* and *To Sail beyond the Sunset*. Pixel has the remarkable ability to appear wherever the narrator of the books happens to be, Heinlein perhaps playing mischievously with the quantum observer theory. The cat is, as the title suggests, able to walk through walls, supposedly because of his 'inability to know any better', and later even develops the ability to talk.

And cats, or, to be more accurate, one cat in particular, inspired another of Heinlein's famous novels. *The Door into Summer* came from a chance remark made by the author's wife, Virginia, when the couple's cat was meowing at the door but refused to go out when the door was opened. It was cold and snowing outside and Virginia suggested that the cat was looking for 'a door into Summer'. This led to the creation of Petronius the Arbiter, Pete for short, a cat who accompanies his owner Daniel Boone Davies on a rather remarkable journey across time.

Davies is an American inventor who is swindled by his fiancée and his business partner, who it turns out have been having an affair behind his back. Kicked out of the company he founded, and somehow losing Pete in the process, he decides, in a fit of despair, to enter suspended animation, a procedure easily available in this version of 1970s' America, and wake up thirty years later. Upon waking he discovers what has happened to his double-crossers and comes up with a cunning plan that makes use of a newly invented time machine to go back in time and get his own back. Most importantly for cat lovers, in doing so he is able to track down Pete and the two are reunited.

The Door into Summer is an enjoyable romp that was both inspired by a cat and features another as a crucial plot device.

Throughout the modern history of literature, science-fiction authors have explored the outer limits of the known and unknown, pushed the boundaries of what is possible in storytelling, taken readers into outer space, onto other planets and into alternative dimensions. It is more than a little comforting to note that they have often done so in the company of cats.

CATS *in* FACT

IN JUNE 2020, THE DEATH OF A CELEBRITY, STAR OF
several books and two feature films, made news headlines
around the world. Broadcasters, from the BBC in the UK to
NHK in Japan, ran moving tributes; obituaries appeared in
newspapers; social media were awash with grief. Of course,
the passing of an international figure is often commemorated
in this way, but this celebrity was a little bit different: it was
a cat. A street cat named Bob.

James Bowen was a recovering drug addict; he had only
recently found a home after a period of rough sleeping
when he came across a stray and injured tomcat near his
flat in Tottenham. Moved by the plight of a creature only
slightly worse off than himself, he took the cat in and nursed
it back to health, using almost all of his small reserve of
cash to pay for food and medical treatment. He named his

new room-mate Bob, because the cat reminded him of the character Killer Bob from the television show *Twin Peaks*, and very soon the two became inseparable.

At the time, Bowen made his living from busking in and around Covent Garden, in London, and he started taking Bob along with him from time to time, the cat sitting on his shoulder while they rode the bus into town together. He soon discovered that his ginger cat was somewhat of a spare-change magnet, with his takings on 'Bob Days' much higher than when he left the cat at home. The attention Bob received was even more marked when Bowen became a *Big Issue* vendor, with customers happily handing over more than the cover price, and often additional gifts for the cat. After a while, once he had relocated to a new pitch near Angel tube station, Bowen found people travelled out of their way to see Bob, and seemed to know his name even though this was their first visit. That was when he discovered that a friendly tourist had uploaded footage of James and Bob to YouTube, and this *Big Issue* seller and his ginger tom had become an Internet sensation. It was shortly after this that a literary agent approached James and suggested there might be a market for a book about this unlikely couple.

That book, *A Street Cat Named Bob*, was published in 2012 and became a global bestseller, selling over 1 million copies in the UK alone and being translated into thirty languages, as well as spawning a number of sequels and two feature films, in which Bob played himself. The reason for the success of that first book is perhaps not immediately apparent when reading it. The writing is fairly pedestrian, and James himself is not always that sympathetic – he repeatedly busks in prohibited areas and feels hard done by when he is moved on by the authorities, and he is suspended as a *Big Issue* seller for a while after he sells copies of the magazine in other vendors' pitches. What stands out, and is almost certainly what has resonated with millions of readers, is the relationship between this troubled man and his cat, and how, through looking after Bob, James manages to turn his own life around. Bob was, if you'll excuse the pun, the catalyst for James's salvation. That redemption story moved many people and is why Bob, when he died, was mourned the world over.

Bob's literary debut is a recent addition to a classification of non-fiction books that could perhaps be described as 'feline biography' – accounts of the lives of cats as written by humans. Examples of these date back through history, sometimes appearing as letters or essays in magazines or pamphlets in the early days of print but occasionally as complete books. A particularly fine example is *La Menagerie Intime*, or *My Private Menagerie*, by Théophile Gautier, a French writer much revered by George Eliot and Oscar Wilde. Published in 1869, the book contains charming and finely observed pen portraits of many of his pets, including several cats. His accounts of Childebrand ('a splendid gutter-cat'), Madame Theophile ('so called because she lived with me on a footing of conjugal intimacy'), Don Pierrot de Navarre ('shared the life of the household with that fullness of satisfaction cats derive from close association with the fireside'), Seraphita ('she spent endless time at her toilet'), Enjolras ('his splendid tail, fluffy as a feather duster'), Gavroche ('a cat with a sharp, satirical look') and Eponine ('her velvety black nose, of as fine a grain as a Perigord truffle')[138] will be recognizable to cat owners centuries later.

CAT PATIENTS

Writing a little less than a century ago was Michael Joseph, who – as well as being the founder of the publishing house that still bears his name, and the man who first published Monica Dickens, H.E. Bates, C.S. Forester and others – was the bestselling author of several books about cats, and his own cats in particular. In *Cat's Company* he writes about cats he grew up with, and later owned as an adult. Perhaps the most poignant story in the book is that of Scissors. Scissors was a 'jolly black and white kitten' that attached itself to Joseph's division in France during the First World War and would 'follow us up the poppy-lined communication trenches and along the front line'. He was fed on bully beef meant for the troops, much to the derisive amusement of the men in the machine-gun section, and caught for himself the occasional rat, which were plentiful in the trenches. When Scissors was hit by shrapnel, Joseph bandaged him up and cared for him until he was better, but the two were parted when the division had to move to another part of the front line at short notice and the cat could not be located in time. Scissors was 'last seen trotting across No-Man's-Land towards the German trenches'.[139]

Joseph's most popular cat book was *Charles: The Story of a Friendship*, published midway through the next world war. The author acquired Charles, a Siamese kitten, in August 1930. He had always wanted to add this breed to his collection and did so while his family were away on holiday. He brought Charles – or, to give him his full name, Charles O'Malley – back to his London house. Joseph, clearly not a home cook, took most of his meals out in local restaurants, smuggling leftovers back for the young kitten. This meant that Charles was fed 'grilled fillets of sole, breast of roast chicken, cream and other delicacies; including, on one occasion, I remember, the best part of duck à la presse'[140] from an early age, and acquired a taste for the finer things in life. These were very different times, as illustrated by the fact that Joseph's only complaint about Charles was that the cat enjoyed playing with 'the staff' so much that when Joseph wanted to introduce his beloved pet to visitors he would often have to summon him up from 'below stairs'.

Man and cat truly bonded, however, when Charles fell ill and Joseph nursed him back to health, just as he did with Scissors decades earlier. From that point on, the cat was almost always at his master's side. Indeed, Joseph took Charles with him when he rejoined the army during the Second World War, the two companions sharing various billets and barracks until Joseph was invalided out and returned home. Charles died at the age of 13, in the arms of his owner.

Charles: The Story of a Friendship captivated readers and sold 40,000 copies in hardback. Elizabeth Bowen, writing in *Tatler*, observed, 'It is, as it claims to be, the straight record of a friendship; and unless you not only hate cats but mistrust friendship, I do not see how the book can possibly leave you cold.' And it is that sense of friendship that pervades the book. If not quite a story of equals, it is certainly one full of love and respect. The author has a wonderful ability to capture the appeal of cats for those that cherish them:

> It is an esoteric cult, this devotion of human beings to the mysterious, graceful, independent, charming and affectionate animals who occupy a unique place in our domestic economy. Unique is the right word, for the cat who lives under our roof and sits by our fire is not a domesticated animal.

And he has a few words to say of those who do not like them:

> There are many who are indifferent to cats. The enlightened felinophile may be forgiven for comparing them with the illiterate who are unable to appreciate the beauties of literature.[141]

Denis O'Connor probably didn't consider himself a felino-phile when, one snowy night in 1966, as a young lecturer at Alnwick College, he was looking out at the Christmas-card scene in his cottage garden and heard the distressed cry of an animal. He walked into the forest in his slippers and found a grey cat caught in a gin trap, an evil device used by gamekeepers to trap animals that might otherwise nab a pheasant or grouse that the landed gentry hoped to shoot at a later date. He released the cat, which was bleeding quite badly, and it shot off into the night. Denis returned home to warm up and dry his feet by the fire, but was overcome with sympathy for the poor creature and ventured back out, with more suitable footwear, and attempted to follow the bloody paw tracks in the snow.

Some time later he tracked the injured animal to an abandoned barn where, close to death, she had found her way back to her two scrawny kittens. He took all three to the local vet, who proclaimed them beyond saving. As the vet went off to prepare the injections that would put them to sleep, Denis stroked one of the kittens, a small black one, and it showed some signs of life. When the vet returned, it was obvious there was no hope for the other two but Denis put the black kitten in his pocket and, to the good-humoured admonishment of the vet, took it home to attempt to save it.

Fashioning a drip feed out of an old fountain-pen ink bladder, Denis fed the kitten, which was clearly near death,

with a mixture of milk, halibut oil, orange juice and aspirin –
perhaps not quite what veterinary science would recommend,
but it worked. Over a period of days, the wee waif started to
move about a bit, grew in strength, and Denis began to hope
that he had saved it. But he was then faced with the problem
of what to do with the tiny creature while he was at work.
Again, his solution was less than orthodox. He took a large
glass jug, lined the bottom with cotton-wool balls and then
placed the kitten inside it. That way it could sit in comfort,
see the world around it, but not escape or come to mischief
while it was still rather frail and vulnerable. This seemed
to work, and Denis would return home to friendly mews
resonating from the jug. And this temporary home also
provided the kitten with a name: Toby Jug.

As Toby grew older it became apparent that he was a
rather distinctive-looking cat with a prominent ruff of fur
across his chest. The vet identified him as a Maine Coon,
though he had never come across a black one before. As
Northumberland in the 1960s was not exactly a Maine
Coon stronghold, it was easy enough to find the only local
breeder and Denis paid her a visit to discover that one of
her beloved cats had gone missing the previous year. By her
description, it was apparent that this was the tragic creature
he had rescued the previous winter. But the source of Toby's
black colour remained a mystery – his mother had not been
pregnant when she had vanished.

As he started to venture out, the young cat became a popular member of the village, apart from when he went through a spell of stealing tomatoes from the neighbours' gardens. Denis took Toby with him on regular camping trips, and even, on one occasion, on a lengthy holiday on horseback, with the cat secured in a saddle bag during the rides. It is clear that the companionship Toby offered was much valued by his owner, who was still a young man and finding his way in the world. So it was a source of distress when, one evening, Toby did not return home from his daily ramblings. Denis found out that the local hunt had passed by earlier in the day and he was worried that Toby had somehow got caught up in the bloody melee. Leaflets were printed and distributed around the village; thankfully, it was only a few days later that Denis received word that a muddy ball of fur had been found at a nearby farm.

When he arrived to reclaim his lost cat, Betty and Joe Green, the owners of Grove Farm, explained how, the day after the hunt, their own cat, Black Bob, had discovered a bedraggled Toby in the barn and had been licking and grooming him, something they found strange because he would usually attack and chase off any other cat that invaded his territory.

'Except for that grey she-cat last Autumn,' Betty cut in. 'They ran together for days on end,' she said.[142]

And then the mystery was solved. Here was Toby Jug, rescued and being cared for by his own father.

Denis and Toby went on to live together in Owl Cottage for another eleven years, until Toby developed a brain tumour, which made him quite unwell and unstable. Dennis realized that the kindest option was to have his friend put to sleep and took him to the veterinary surgery. But when the vet left the room to get the required injection, Toby snuggled against Denis and climbed into his coat pocket, just as he had when he was rescued as a kitten. Denis decided that his friend should die at the home they shared together and the two of them headed back. Toby was buried in the garden. Denis promised, at the graveside, to write their story one day, which he did nearly thirty years later, in *Paw Tracks in the Moonlight*. It is a genuinely heart-warming and moving tale of a lengthy friendship.

So far, the books in this chapter have opened with a cat being found, rescued or acquire. The appeal of this sort of story may well lie in the sense that, as a reader, you are witness to the 'birth', life and, in some cases, death of the feline protagonist as the book progresses. It is easy to become emotionally invested when you are sharing important moments from a life, and from a relationship between animal and human, when they are conveyed with a sense of respect, love and humour, as is certainly the case with the writing of Joseph and O'Connor.

I & Claudius, by Clare de Vries, is somewhat different. In this book, Claudius, the feline subject of its pages, is already 19 years old when the story begins. He is, unless he plans to break a Guinness World Record, fairly near the end of his life and the reader's time is spent with him in that knowledge.

Clare is in her early twenties. Her mother has recently died and she is going through, if not quite a quarter-life crisis, then certainly a bit of a troubled time. She has long harboured a desire to drive across America and this may be the ideal time to embark upon that adventure. The problem is that she is stuck in London with the elderly family cat she has now inherited. Some people would find a new home for the cat and head off to the States. Others might postpone their dream until a more convenient time. De Vries does neither. Instead, she decides to take Claudius with her.

You see, Clare grew up with Claudius and cannot remember a time without him. He was there throughout her childhood, available to be stroked in moments of sadness, present during many landmarks in her life, and was even sitting in her bedroom on the night she lost her virginity. The idea of dumping him to go travelling is incomprehensible to her. If she is going to drive across an entire continent, she wants him in the passenger seat. A male feline Thelma to her Louise.

And that is precisely what happens. She ships over her battered old Lancia, intending to use it as her mode of transport, but it breaks down while she is still in New York. She has to buy a new car – well, new to her – and invests in a second-hand Buick. This chunky machine becomes their carriage, and together she and Claudius set off along the freeways and highways of America.

Of course, travelling with a cat over such a long distance is not without its complications. De Vries installs a litter tray in the passenger seat well, which Claudius is quite happy to use, but she has to keep the windows open in all weathers unless she wants to live with the smell. Her plan is to stay in cheap motels, to keep the costs down, but many of these do not allow pets, and certainly not cats, so there is a fair deal of fibbing and smuggling going on. More than once she gets caught, and more than once she is unceremoniously evicted. An elderly cat will sometimes get ill and need medical attention, which can be expensive in a country where free, or even cheap, health care for humans, let alone animals, is seen as an evil communist plan.

Despite these potential drawbacks, Clare and Claudius do make it, slowly and surely, across the country, stopping off to see the sights along the way. They visit the Grand Canyon, where midway through a donkey trek Claudius is discovered in her bag to the horror of the guide, as pets are certainly not permitted, and she is sent packing. They check out two different Las Vegases, after de Vries turns up at the one in New Mexico only to discover that it isn't the Vegas with the neon lights, cabaret singers and slot machines. Trips to Graceland and New Orleans are less eventful, although de Vries does try voodoo medicine on Claudius when he falls ill there. At a rodeo in Dallas someone offers Clare $10,000 for the cat simply because he is such a beautiful specimen, and presumably because they have more money than sense. It is an offer that would solve her financial problems in one fell swoop, but that isn't accepted. What is accepted is nearly every offer of a meal, a drink or a room for the night, no matter who extends the invitation. This will lead some readers to yell *What are you thinking?* at the page as De Vries goes off with some dodgy-looking fella who has a sofa she can sleep on. There are a few close calls, but she comes out unscathed.

This is a journey of joy and risk, of free abandon, of new beginnings and, sadly, of endings. De Vries sets out on her journey knowing that Claudius probably won't survive their visit, and she certainly has no intention of putting him into quarantine on their return (this being the 1990s and an age before cat passports). Sure enough, by the time they reach Los Angeles, Claudius is on his last legs and his kidneys are failing. Claire sells the Buick, buys tickets back to New York; it is there, after one false start when she can't go through with it, that she has Claudius put down.

I & Claudius certainly contains more swearing, sex scenes and hangovers than any of the other books mentioned here, but it is a welcome addition to our library for precisely that reason. Cat biographies are often designed to make readers emit a quiet *ahh* or *aww*, so it is refreshing to come across one with a bit more edge to it, and more likely to elicit an *argh*.

CATS AT WORK

One quite specific type of cat biography that is clearly intended to prompt a happy sigh is what we could class as the 'cat in workplace' book. In recent years, bookshops have become inundated with tales of cats in locations where they would not normally be found.

Sometimes these are grouped together in illustrated photo books containing anecdotes about *London Pubcats*, *Cathedral Cats* or *Shop Cats of New York*. These may make for entertaining reading in the dentist's waiting room, but there are also more detailed stories about specific cats that have captured the hearts of the communities in which they live. *Felix the Railway Cat* tells the tale of a kitten adopted by the staff of Huddersfield train station (once called 'the most splendid in Britain' by John Betjeman) after months of badgering their station manager for permission. Felix is a little tentative at first but eventually finds the confidence to patrol every platform and, in doing so, win the affection of passengers who travel the TransPennine Express route. Like Bob, she (having been given her name when the staff thought she was a tomcat, only to be proved wrong) became an Internet celebrity and rail travellers from all over the world would stop off at Huddersfield to catch a glimpse of this famous station cat.

Another cat that achieved worldwide fame was Dewey Readmore Books, the resident cat at the public library in Spencer, Iowa. Having been abandoned in the library's dropbox as a kitten in 1987, he was cared for by one of the librarians, Vicki Myron, who named him after Melvil Dewey, inventor of the Dewey Decimal Classification System. His additional names were added after a public vote. He stayed at the library for nearly twenty years, during which time his notoriety grew as a result of several news reports and television shows. When he died in 2006 his obituary appeared in 170 publications.

Factual books about cats are rarely going to win literary awards, but that isn't the point of them. They appeal because they explore the centuries-old bond between humans and felines, something that most readers of these books will have experienced and can relate to. They want to be reminded of their own cats, to recognize themselves and their pets in the pages, to be entertained and moved.

It would take a heart of steel to remain unmoved by our last book in this chapter, *Homer's Odyssey* by Gwen Cooper.

When a Miami vet is presented with a two-week-old stray kitten with such a serious eye infection that both eyes have to be removed, she knows it might be kinder to put it out of its misery, but she is also aware that the cat could survive and live a perfectly healthy, if somewhat hindered life, with a bit of help. Determined to find someone to adopt it, despite many rejections, she finally persuades Gwen Cooper, a client with two cats already, to take him in.

This generous adoption is even more remarkable when you consider that Cooper had just left a serious relationship and didn't have a permanent home at the time – she was being put up by a friend until she could find somewhere to live. But she knew why she had to look after this blind cat.

> I wanted to believe there could be something within you that was so essential and so courageous that nothing – no boyfriend, no employer, no trauma – could tarnish or rob you of it.[143]

At a low point in her own life, she needed to be reminded that there was a strength inside everyone, even this tiny defenceless creature. And although *tiny* remained true for a while, *defenceless* was soon shrugged off as, despite his lack of sight, the kitten, now named Homer after the blind poet of Ancient Greece, was climbing up curtains, scaling bookcases and pouncing on Cooper's other cats, Scarlett and Vashti, with vim and vigour. He even, at one point, scares off a burglar.

Two scenes in *Homer's Odyssey* really stand out. The first is Cooper's realization that Homer uses his miaows to communicate in a way her other cats do not. He has an entire repertoire that seems to mean different things – *Is this OK? Are you still there? I need help* – and she reminds herself that Homer has always been blind so he has no concept that other people, or cats, can see him. He assumes everyone experiences the world the same way he does, so uses sound to navigate that world and to let other creatures know where he is.

The second takes place on 11 September 2001, a date most will recall. Cooper had just arrived at work, in her new home city of New York, when the attack on the Twin Towers took place. Her apartment, containing three cats, was on the thirty-first floor of a building rather close to the tragic events and while her natural instinct was to get home as soon as possible to check on and care for her pets, there was no way of doing that. For several days, army and police cordoned off the area near Ground Zero and an increasingly panicked Cooper tried to find ways to rescue her pets. The way she eventually did so is a welcome reminder of the nature of human kindness, but we won't reveal this particular spoiler here.

You cannot spend time in the company of Homer, even at the remove of the printed page, without being impressed by his sheer force of will. Here is a cat that won't allow anything to stop him, especially the small matter of having no eyes. It is a wonderful example of how a biography of a cat can speak to the heart of a human, and that is what the very best of these books will do.

CATS *in* TRANSLATION

C ATS FEATURE IN NOVELS AND STORIES ACROSS
the world. With the exception of the impressive
polyglots among you, most readers are reliant on the
wonderful work of translators, and the publishers that
support them, to make those stories accessible. And if you
are British, then you are probably more reliant on translators
than most, according to a European Commission survey that
showed that 62 per cent of us can speak *only* English.[144] Sadly,
this means that a wealth of international literature remains
unobtainable. However, an increasing number of books are
being translated into English, and we have sought out a small
number that feature our feline friends.

JAPAN

We start our journey, perhaps a little inauspiciously, in a car park outside an apartment block in suburban Tokyo. A cat with no name, a stray, weaves through the parked cars each day in search of food – food which Satoru, a young man who lives in one of the apartments, regularly leaves for him. One morning, however, the cat is a little less careful than normal, perhaps complacent in the knowledge that a meal is just moments away, and gets hit by a car as he crosses the road. Satoru discovers the injured cat, takes him in, cares for him and gives him a name: Nana (the cat's tail is shaped like a number seven, and 'nana' is Japanese for 'seven'). The two become friends.

In *The Travelling Cat Chronicles* by Hiro Arikawa, translated by Philip Gabriel, Nana's story is narrated by the cat himself, a cat not entirely enamoured by his new name, which he thinks would be better suited to a female of the species. Nana is a wonderful creation, and an engaging narrator, with Arikawa (along with Gabriel) capturing what many readers will consider to be the essence of the unlikely relationship between humans and cats: the co-dependency, the occasional bickering, the one-way conversations that each is convinced the other understands. This particular relationship comes into its own as Nana and Satoru's story progresses.

After five years together, some unexpected and unwelcome news (we shall not spoil the plot by revealing more, but you can probably guess) means that Satoru needs to find a new owner for Nana. He doesn't want to hand him over to just anyone, though, and is keen that Nana is comfortable in his next home, so the two companions jump into a battered old silver van and travel to 'interview' various friends and acquaintances from Satoru's past, all potential candidates to adopt Nana.

Satoru hopes their first port of call, the home of his childhood friend Kosuke, will prove to be sufficient. After all, when they were kids he and Kosuke bonded over a stray cat named Haichi (Japanese for 'eight'); if his old friend were to adopt Nana, things would come full circle. But Nana has other ideas. He senses that the real reason Kosuke is prepared to adopt him is to attempt to win back his estranged wife, and that strikes him as a doomed venture, so he hisses and bares his teeth and refuses to leave the cat box to meet his new owner. Accepting their failure, Satoru and Nana move on to another potential home, and then another, with each stop on their journey revealing a further episode from Satoru's past until his story is more or less complete, and each stop also proving unsatisfactory to Nana in some way – he is handled too roughly, there is already a dog in the house, seemingly any excuse to not be parted from his friend.

Eventually, the reason Satoru needs to find someone to look after Nana and the solution to that problem combine to offer a heartwarming, and heartbreaking, ending. *The*

Travelling Cat Chronicles is a novel that examines the friendship between cats and their 'owners'. It does so by presenting both the positive and the negative aspects and manages to avoid too much sentimentality along the way.

If there is such a thing as feline literature – and we have spent many pages trying to convince you that there is – then it is fair to say that Japan is very much at the forefront of it. The Japanese affection for cats is responsible for one of the most widely recognized decorative items in the world – the Maneki-Neko, or 'beckoning cat'. The cute figurines depict a Japanese bobtail cat with one paw raised in a typical Japanese beckoning gesture. There are different origin stories behind this popular figure – one that a cat saved the life of a samurai by beckoning him to move, just before a bolt of lightning struck. The samurai began to worship at the temple where the cat lived, ensuring the temple's survival. Another claims that the cat helped a shop thrive. A more controversial account claims that the cat replaced the phallic symbol which used to mark the entrance of brothels. It has even been rumoured that the Maneki-Neko was the inspiration for Hello Kitty, one of Japan's most famous and enduring brands.[145]

Japan is clearly a country which prizes cats highly. It is the birthplace of the cat café – cafés containing cats for patrons to stroke and hang out with – and there are several cat islands where feline inhabitants outnumber the humans, sometimes by eight to one. This affection for cats has long been represented in Japanese literature, but in recent years the trend has exploded. In the ten years since 2007, more than 5,400 books about cats were published in Japan. To put that in perspective, that is more than were published about Buddhism, baseball (another national obsession) or the country's favourite drink, sake.

One Japanese author notorious for including cats in his work is perhaps the most famous of all: Haruki Murakami. So famous is his cat obsession that the *New York Times* once printed a 'Murakami Bingo' cartoon by Grant Snider, listing his common themes and images, including 'Unexpected Phone Call' and 'Mysterious Woman', but also no fewer than three feline entries: 'Cats', 'Speaking to Cats' and 'Vanishing Cats'.

Murakami's first major international bestseller, *The Wind-up Bird Chronicle*, translated by Jay Rubin, begins with the narrator, Toru Okada, an unemployed lawyer's assistant, being tasked by his wife Kumiko to find their missing cat. This initial quest provokes a series of events that become more and more surreal, and soon involve the disappearance of Kumiko herself. Without the cat, there is no novel.

Cats feature even more prominently in the plot of Murakami's 2002 novel *Kafka on the Shore*, translated by Philip Gabriel, as well as on nearly every cover of the book no matter what country or language it is published in. The title character, Kafka Tamura, a runaway teen, can't pass a cat without stopping to pet it, but it is Satoru Nakata, the protagonist of a parallel narrative, who is the real cat lover. As a child, Nakata was involved in a mysterious incident. Towards the end of the Second World War he was on a school trip to pick mushrooms when a blinding flash in the sky rendered everyone unconscious. Most of the kids and teachers awoke shortly afterwards, but Nakata was out cold for weeks. When he woke he had lost many of his mental faculties, but they had been replaced with the ability to communicate with cats. Now, as an adult, he makes a living by locating missing cats for their owners, something he can do by questioning other cats in the neighbourhood. The reader is treated to an array of talking cats, which in typical Murakami fashion prove to be crucial to the weird and wonderful plot.

It is hard to find a Murakami novel that doesn't include cats, and he has also written several short stories and essays about them. He has spoken in interviews about how cats have been constant companions throughout his life. In the 1970s, before his writing days, he and his wife owned a jazz club named Peter Cat after their favourite pet. A decade or so later, when he was a few novels into his career as a writer, he asked someone he knew at a publishing house to look after his current cat while he was away. In return he offered to write a book for them. That book turned out to be *Norwegian Wood*, the best-selling novel in Japanese history. Clearly, Murakami has a love and respect for cats that find their way into his writing, and yet he refuses point blank to read any meaning into this – no metaphor or deeper textual analysis – apart from the fact that he just likes cats, which seems like a good enough reason.

Takashi Hiraide's *The Guest Cat* explores the potential for a deep connection between cats and humans. Translated by Eric Selland, the novel introduces us to a couple who are renting a small cottage where they spend their days working from home. A case of shingles has convinced the husband to quit his job in publishing and become a freelancer, while his wife is a proofreader, but they have concerns as to whether they can afford to live on their incomes in the long run. Their life is quiet; there is a sense of disconnect from the external world, as well as between husband and wife. Triggered by the passing of a friend, the man ponders 'the tide that can suddenly pull you out, beyond the shallows, into the sea of hardship, and even death'.[146] Into this atmosphere, marked by uncertainty about the future and a lack of direction, enters the guest cat of the title – Chibi. She belongs to the neighbour's son, but the couple soon meet her as she explores their cottage's garden: 'Chibi was a jewel of a cat. Her pure white fur was mottled with several lampblack blotches containing just a bit of light brown.'[147]

Chibi becomes a regular visitor, eventually even being given access to the house. Her presence seems to give the couple a new energy, making them laugh and motivating them to complete work projects. The slim volume is filled with beautiful and detailed descriptions of the cat's behaviour, expressing how much the couple appreciate her.

> Her figure, balanced on a branch at the top of the persimmon tree she had dashed up, carefully gauging the wind, bracing herself for its next movements, seemed to have separated itself from both heaven and earth, projected into a space that was ultimately dimensionless.[148]

Even after she is no longer part of their life, Chibi leaves a lasting impression, having changed how the couple view the world around them, leaving them more receptive to the beauty that surrounds us on a daily basis.

Another Japanese writer, Genki Kawamura, sends a strong signal about the importance of cats in his novel's title – *If Cats Disappeared from the World*, also translated by Selland. The narrator, a young man, one day finds out that he is suffering from a brain tumour and has mere months to live. As he is trying to process this information, the Devil appears in his apartment and proposes a deal: he gains an additional day in the world of the living by making something disappear from the world. This being the Devil, it is of course not the narrator who gets to decide what will disappear, but his evil counterpart. The deal is agreed and the narrator has to come to terms with some big changes in the world – phones and movies disappearing, even clocks. But when the Devil suggests that cats should disappear from the world, the narrator simply cannot agree to this because there is Cabbage, his cat, who has been his constant companion and source of affection and comfort. Even in the most desperate times, from the death of his mother to his struggle to accept his fate, Cabbage has been there for him. As much as the novel is a contemplation of life and mortality, it is also a love letter to cats and how they sometimes help us to be open to the possibility of love.

CATS AND CONFLICTS

If we now leave Japan for Europe, we find Muri, a cat with a rather unsentimental attitude towards humans. He finds himself alone when the family of humans he lives with flee their home at short notice. To the reader, the abandonment is understandable: this is Sarajevo and Yugoslavia has just exploded into civil war. Muri, however, is uncomprehending and furious: 'I need my bowl, my blanket and my people to serve me.'[149] Cat owners will perhaps recognize a common feline attitude here. In Muri, Russian author Ilya Boyashov has created an authentic personality for his hero, and Amanda Love Darragh's translation certainly captures that voice.

The somewhat miffed Muri then proceeds to embark on what turns out to be a philosophical journey across half of Europe as he tries to track down his 'servants'. At each stop he meets, and often befriends, a different human and we get a snapshot of that human's life – such as an astronomer determined to record a supernova despite the war going on outside the doors of the observatory, or an Austrian mayor who has an epiphany about the state of the world – as well as a development of the book's main theme: is it the destination that matters, or the journey itself? *The Way of Muri* is like an episode of *The Littlest Hobo* but written by Ralph Waldo Emerson. Importantly for our circumnavigation, it covers a lot of cat miles along the way.

Whilst the previous stories give the feline character the role of narrator, the next novel takes a very different approach. In Finnish author Pajtim Statovci's wonderfully strange and moving *My Cat Yugoslavia* (translated by David Hackston), the central character is a young gay man called Bekim, who meets the titular cat in a Finnish gay bar, of all places. In a surreal twist, this cat, whose name we never learn and who remains a mystery throughout the novel, is a talking, even singing, cat who walks on two legs and charms Bekim with his impressive physique and glossy fur. It comes as a shock that the cat soon reveals itself to be a homophobic, nasty fellow. Bekim is in a vulnerable state – a refugee who, as a child, fled Kosovo during the war and came to Finland, he is painfully aware of being the eternal outsider. With the 'wrong' name, the 'wrong' accent, the 'wrong' sexuality, he remains a social outcast. Even his family rejected him, unable to cope with his sheer otherness, which, among other things, manifested itself in a morbid fear of snakes. Learning that Bekim decides to buy a boa constrictor as a pet, despite his debilitating fear of the creatures, goes some way to illustrate just how fiercely he is battling his own demons.

All the while, the cat forces himself into Bekim's life, and begins to exploit his host's vulnerability, belittling and ridiculing him, making constant demands and in no way returning the love and admiration which Bekim feels for him. We are left to ponder the role of the cat in this sad story. He seems to be a contradiction in himself – singing and dancing in a gay bar but despising homosexuality, making fun of Bekim's sheer weirdness, whilst clearly being a freak of nature himself. These strange contradictions mirror Bekim's struggle to accept himself for who he is. The cat's outrageous and confusing behaviour challenges Bekim to finally confront the demons which have haunted his young life, and eventually put them to rest. *My Cat Yugoslavia* charts a surreal, turbulent, but also often heartbreaking journey, which ultimately leads Bekim to the longed-for inner peace and fulfilment.

CATS IN CONTROL

The next novel lightens the mood and introduces another witty cat narrator, the hilariously named Sugar Zach.

Written by Greek author Lena Divani and translated by Konstantine Matsoukas, *Seven Lives and One Great Love: Memoirs of a Cat* commences as Zach enters the world for his seventh life, reincarnated as a fluffy white furball, although he is by no means as innocent as his appearance might suggest. Zach's previous lives have provided him with a wealth of experience, a collection of cat words of wisdom and a general sense of benevolent superiority over the human race. One could say that Zach initially talks about humans as we might find ourselves speaking about cats – their quirky habits and general cluelessness exasperate and entertain him, whilst he shows great confidence in his ability to manipulate their behaviour with his carefully laid out plans.

It is important to understand that, due to his sixth incarnation as a library cat, he accumulated an impressive literary knowledge and, what's more, a true passion for the written word. It's not surprising therefore that he tells us about the fate of William Burroughs's and Sylvia Plath's cats as he discusses his endeavour to find the perfect human parent for his next life. Zach sees his fate fulfilled when he meets the Damsel, a writer, and skilfully engineers his adoption. He is intrigued by writers – he has devoured their works, but what about the business of writing? In his usual shrewd manner he quickly grasps that the Damsel is no easy target, but his previous lives have taught him many a lesson on how to worm his way into a human's life. And he is determined to leave his underwhelming and common family behind, convinced that he is destined for greater things and plusher surroundings. As the relationship between Zach and the Damsel develops, he reveals himself to be a skilled chronicler of the human condition, fulfilling the function of storyteller with which he is so fascinated. His humorous take on the Damsel's love life soon takes on a touchingly caring and protective tone. It becomes clear that the most successful relationship in the Damsel's life is with Zach himself. Although Zach berates the Damsel for some of the choices she makes in her life, he ultimately comes to love her, in spite or maybe because of her very human flaws. Divani achieves a rare feat – to write a cat story, which is heart-warming and funny, without the sickly sweet tinge that would overshadow the thoroughly cattish and entertaining tone.

We have already explored the cat as a symbol of personal struggles in *My Cat Yugoslavia*. The theme continues in a story by celebrated French writer Colette. We saw Colette's love for her feline companions in a previous chapter. Her affinity with cats is reflected in much of her writing, but takes centre stage in her lesser known short story 'The Cat', translated by Antonia White. The cat in question is Saha, who belongs to Alain, an only child now grown up and about to marry beautiful and energetic Camille. Saha has been with Alain for a number of years, firmly establishing herself in his life before his engagement. We learn about Saha only from

Alain's and Camille's observations, which could not be more different. Alain simply adores Saha, for her feline beauty, for her at times mischievous, at times loving nature, and ultimately for her loyalty to him. Saha will come when he calls and he will do as she pleases – feeding her tasty morsels, playing with her.

A basic, but fulfilling relationship it appears to the reader, but to Alain Saha clearly is more than a pet. His fiancée Camille is not as enamoured by Saha and it quickly becomes apparent why she might feel this way. Alain seems to harbour deeper feelings for Saha than for Camille, accepting Saha's flaws with tolerance and unconditional love, whereas he is quick to judge Camille and her shortcomings more harshly. He physically desires Camille, but he cannot bring himself to accept that she might have flaws and that they might have disagreements – the characteristics of a quite average relationship between two adults. Instead, he escapes to his childhood home, spending time with his beloved Saha, in an environment which envelopes Alain with a warmth and familiarity that he cannot find in his marital life.

Saha comes to represent Alain's deep attachment to his childhood home and his life as a carefree young man, which he is loath to lose. When he realizes that Saha is unhappy living away from him, not eating and increasingly lethargic, he decides to take her away to his temporary marital home. Initially, this strange 'love triangle' continues relatively peacefully. Alain relishes Saha's presence, taking pleasure in having her close when he returns home in the evenings and occasionally even seeking out her company at night, rather than sharing a bed with his wife. Soon Camille and Alain's relationship becomes more and more fractious, and in turn tension between Camille and Saha rises, resulting in Camille taking desperate action, with far-reaching consequences. More than ever before, it becomes clear that Saha, with everything she represents, has a firm hold on Alain and he admits to himself that only her death will enable him to move on.

Our whistle-stop journey has included cats as narrators, cats as metaphors, cats as observers, cats as companions and cats as guides, but there are numerous other examples of feline fiction from all manner of countries and cultures that are worthy of exploration. We hope this small selection has whetted your appetite for more feline fiction in translation.

AFTERWORD

The idea for this book was born out of 'Around the World in 10 Cats', an event we hosted at the British Library, complementing their *Cats on the Page* exhibition in 2018. Here, we took the audience on a literary journey around the world, uncovering cats in translated fictions from across the globe. With the encouragement from Bodleian Library Publishing, this initial foray into the world of literary felines inspired us to delve deeper into the rich and complex treasure trove of cats in literature (and you will have met some of the international representatives in 'Cats in Translation').

We hope you enjoyed your journey through the world of literary felines, as much as we enjoyed discovering them on the pages of so many different books. As we occasionally point out in the course of the previous chapters, this book by no means presents you with an exhaustive list of cats in literature. Our intention was to explore as many different genres and perspectives on literary felines as possible, hence we had to limit the number of books we were able to touch on in each chapter.

As we hinted in our introduction, there is more to discover, and we hope that you feel encouraged to do so. Perhaps you will pay close attention, when reading your next book, as to whether there is a cat hiding in plain sight, among the human characters. Perhaps you will return to some of your favourite stories to find out whether a cat might have played their part in shaping the plot.

And perhaps you will look at your cat at home in a new light – could they inspire the next literary bestseller?

NOTES

1. K.M. Rogers, *Cat*, Reaktion Books, London, 2019, p. 14; D. Engels, *Classical Cats*, Routledge, Abingdon, 2001, p. 21; A. Diesel, 'Felines and Female Divinities: The Association of Cats with Goddesses, Ancient and Contemporary', *Journal for the Study of Religion*, vol. 21, no. 1, 2008, p. 79.
2. L.A. Vocelle, *Revered and Reviled: A Complete History of the Domestic Cat*, Great Cat Publications, 2017, p. 13.
3. Rogers, *Cat*, p. 15; Diesel, 'Felines and Female Divinities', p. 79.
4. Engels, *Classical Cats*, pp. 21–2.
5. Diesel, 'Felines and Female Divinities', pp. 78–9; Engels, *Classical Cats*, pp. 7, 23–5; Rogers, *Cat*, p. 8; Vocelle, *Revered and Reviled*, pp. 15–16.
6. J.A. Serpell, 'Domestication and History of the Cat', in Dennis C. Turner and Patrick Bateson (eds), *The Domestic Cat*, Cambridge University Press, Cambridge, 2013, pp. 90–92; Engels, *Classical Cats*, pp. 29–30, 32.
7. Diesel, 'Felines and Female Divinities', pp. 85–6; Engels, *Classical Cats*, pp. 32, 55–7, 79; Rogers, *Cat*, pp. 18–21; Vocelle, *Revered and Reviled*, pp. 53–5.
8. J. Mann, *From Aesop to Reynard: Beast Literature in Medieval Britain*, Oxford University Press, Oxford, 2009, pp. 3–4.
9. Aesop, *The Aesop for Children*, illus. M. Winter, Rand McNally, Chicago, 1919, p. 89.
10. Aesop, *Aesop's Fables*, 2011, Project Gutenberg, www.gutenberg.org/cache/epub/28/pg28.html, fable 72; accessed 23 June 2021.
11. Aesop, *Aesop's Fables*, trans. V.S. Vernon Jones, Avenel Books, New York, 1912.
12. J.W. Goethe, *Reynard the Fox*, John C. Nimmo, London, 1887.
13. F. Edgerton, *The Panchatantra Reconstructed*, American Oriental Society,

New Haven CT, 1924, pp. 369–71.

14. Rogers, *Cat*, p. 26.
15. Vocelle, *Revered and Reviled*, pp. 90–91.
16. Engels, *Classical Cats*, pp. 150–51.
17. C. Nizamoglu, 'Cats in Islamic Culture', 2007, *Muslim Heritage*, https://muslimheritage.com/cats-islamic-culture/#ftn111; accessed 23 June 2021.
18. Rogers, *Cats*, p. 24
19. M. Bunson, *The Vampire Encyclopedia*, Gramercy Books, New York, 1993, p. 184; M.E. Opler, 'Japanese Folk Belief Concerning the Cat', *Journal of the Washington Academy of Sciences*, vol. 35, no. 9, 1945, pp. 269–75.
20. J. Piggott, *Japanese Mythology*, Paul Hamlyn, London, 1969, p. 72.
21. Engels, *Classical Cats*, pp. 140–41, 158, 163; Serpell, 'Domestication and History of the Cat', p. 97; Vocelle, *Revered and Reviled*, pp. 74, 110.
22. Engels, *Classical* Cats, pp. 152, 157–9; Rogers, *Cats*, pp. 26–7, 54–5; Vocelle, *Revered and Reviled*, pp. 106–9, 132–50.
23. M. Nikolajeva, 'Devils, Demons, Familiars, Friends: Towards a Semiotics of Literary Cats', *Marvels & Tales*, vol. 23, no. 2, 20098, p. 251; Engels, *Classical Cats*, p. 171; Rogers, *Cats*, p. 81.
24. C. Perrault, 'Puss in Boots', in Becky Brown (ed.), *Classic Cat Stories*, Macmillan, London, 2020, p. 141.
25. T. Capote, *Breakfast at Tiffany's*, Penguin, London, 2000, p. 20.
26. Ibid., p. 35.
27. D. Lessing, 'An Old Woman and Her Cat', in Diana Secker Tesdell (ed.), *Cat Stories*, Everyman, New York, 2011, p. 68.
28. E.A. Poe, 'The Black Cat', in Tesdall (ed.), *Cat Stories*, p. 205.
29. Ibid., p. 206.
30. Ibid.
31. Ibid., p. 212.
32. Ibid., p. 216.
33. C. Dickens, *Bleak House*, Hurd & Houghton, New York, 1869, p. 170.
34. Ibid., pp. 87–90.
35. M. Bulgakov, *The Master and Margarita*, Vintage, London, 2004, p. 63.
36. Ibid., p. 146.
37. Ibid., p. 292.
38. S. King, *Pet Sematary*, Hodder & Stoughton, London, 1989, p. 45.
39. Ibid., p. 21.
40. F. Leiber, 'Space-Time for Springers', in Bill Fawcett (ed.), *Cats in Space and Other Places*, Simon & Schuster, New York, 1992, p. 160.
41. S. Jackson, *We Have Always Lived in the Castle*, Penguin, London, 2009, p. 53.
42. C. Dickens, *The Uncommercial Traveller*, Chapman & Hall, London, 1905, ch. 10.
43. C. Dickens, *Great Expectations*, Alma Books, Richmond, 2014, p. 155.

44. C. Dickens, 2006, *The Life and Adventures of Nicholas Nickleby*, Macmillan, London, 1916, ch. 49.

45. Ibid., ch. 42.

46. C. Dickens, *The Personal History of David Copperfield*, University Society Publishers, New York, 1908, p. 153.

47. T. Hardy, *Tess of the d'Urbervilles*, Macmillan, London, 1912, ch. 27; www.gutenberg.org/files/110/110-h/110-h.htm.

48. B. Stoker, *Dracula*, Penguin Books, London, 2003, p. 225.

49. V. Woolf, *Between the Acts*, Vintage, London, 1992, p. 62.

50. V. Woolf, *A Room of One's Own*, Oxford University Press, Oxford, 2015, p. 10.

51. É. Zola, *Nana*, Penguin, London, 1972, p. 166.

52. Ibid., p. 170.

53. A. Brontë, *Agnes Grey*, Thomas Cautley Newby, London, 1847, ch. 11.

54. J. Swift, *Gulliver's Travels*, Lerner, Minneapolis MN, 2015, p. 103.

55. D.H. Lawrence, *Women in Love*, Cambridge University Press, Cambridge, 1987, p. 148.

56. Ibid., p. 150.

57. Ibid., p. 300

58. F.S. Fitzgerald, *The Great Gatsby*, Penguin, London, 2000, p. 25.

59. F. Dostoevsky, *Crime and Punishment*, Lerner, Minneapolis MN, 2015, p. 2.

60. É. Zola, *Thérèse Raquin*, Vintage, London, 2014, p. 39.

61. Ibid., p. 133.

62. D.H. Lawrence, *Lady Chatterley's Lover*, Arcadia, London, 2013, p. 93.

63. M. Twain, *The Adventures of Tom Sawyer*, Samizdat Press, Orange CT, p. 96.

64. Ibid., p. 99.

65. L.M. Alcott, *Little Women*, Xist Classics, Tustin CA, 2014, p. 33.

66. Ibid., p. 140.

67. G. Orwell, *Animal Farm*, Mariner, Boston MA, 1989, p. 11.

68. Ibid., p. 14.

69. J. Joyce, *Ulysses*, Booklassic, Csorna, 2015, p. 71.

70. Ibid., p. 72.

71. J. Tanizaki, *A Cat, A Man, and Two Women*, Daunt, London, 2017, p. 13.

72. *The Mahābhārata*, trans. Kisari Mohan Ganguli, 1883–96, www.gutenberg.org/cache/epub/15476/pg15476.html.

73. 'Pangur Bán', http://irisharchaeology.ie/2013/10/pangur-ban.

74. C. Smart, 'My Cat Jeoffry', www.poetryfoundation.org/poems/45173/jubilate-agno.

75. W. Cowper, 'The Retired Cat', www.luminarium.org/eightlit/cowper/cat.htm.

76. J. Baillie, 'The Kitten', www.poetrynook.com/poem/kitten-0.

77. T. Hardy, 'Last Words to a Dumb Friend', www.poemhunter.com/

poem/last-words-to-a-dumb-friend.

78. T. Gray, 'Ode on the Death of a Favourite Cat Drowned in a Tub of Goldfishes', www.poetryfoundation.org/poems/44302/ode-on-the-death-of-a-favourite-cat-drowned-in-a-tub-of-goldfishes.

79. C. Aberconway (ed.), *Dictionary of Cat Lovers*, Michael Joseph, London, 1949, p. 75.

80. Ibid., p. 98.

81. G. Ewart, 'A 14 year old Convalescent Cat in the Winter', https://poetryarchive.org/poem/14-year-old-convalescent-cat-winter.

82. M. Atwood, 'Mourning for Cats', in *The Door*, Virago, London, 2009, p. 44.

83. H. Heine, 'Songs of Creation', in *The Poems of Heine*, George Bell and Sons, London, 1908; www.gutenberg.org/files/52882/52882-h/52882-h.htm.

84. R. Herrick, 'A Country Life', www.luminarium.org/sevenlit/herrick/thomas.htm.

85. R. Herrick, 'His Grange, or Private Wealth', www.luminarium.org/sevenlit/herrick/grange.htm.

86. G. Apollinaire, 'The Cat', https://thefirelizard.wordpress.com/tag/guillaume-apollinaire.

87. H. Munro, 'Milk for the Cat', www.poemhunter.com/poem/milk-for-the-cat.

88. W.H. Davies, 'The Cat', www.poetryexplorer.net/poem.php?id=10024954.

89. B.W. Aldiss, *The Cat Improvement Co.*, Green Cat Press, Salt Lake City UT, 2004.

90. Aberconway (ed.), *Dictionary of Cat Lovers*, p. 143.

91. K. Hale, *Orlando the Marmalade Cat: A Camping Holiday*, Puffin, London, 2014, p. 3.

92. J. Kerr, *Mog the Forgetful Cat*, William Collins, London, 1970.

93. J. Kerr, *Creatures*, HarperCollins, London, 2013, p. 153.

94. S. Kitamura, 'Me and My Cat', www.youtube.com/watch?v=eDzISc6o_Xs.

95. J. Donaldson, *Tabby McTat*, illus. A. Scheffler, Alison Green Books, London, 2009.

96. Dr. Seuss, *The Cat in the Hat*, HarperCollins, London, 2017.

97. N. Gaiman, *Coraline*, Bloomsbury, London, 2013, p. 45.

98. B. Sleigh, *Carbonel*, Puffin, London, 2015, p. 31.

99. Ibid., p. 119.

100. S.F. Said, *Varjak Paw*, illus. D. McKean, Corgi Books, London, 2014.

101. E. Hunter, *Warrior Cats: Into the Wild*, HarperCollins, London, 2003.

102. M. Ende, *The Night of Wishes: Or the Satanarchaeolidealcohellish Notion Potion*, trans. H. Schwarzbauer and R. Takvorian, illus. R. Kehn, New York Review, New York, 2017.

103. M. Morpurgo, *Kaspar, Prince of Cats*, HarperCollins, London, 2010, p. 15.

104. L. Carroll, *Alice's Adventures in Wonderland*, illus. J. Tenniel, Maynard, Merrill, New York, 1895, p. 44.

105. S. Collins, *The Hunger Games*, Scholastic, London, 2013, p. 3.
106. R. Kipling, 'The Cat that Walked by Himself', in Becky Brown (ed.), *Classic Cat Stories*, Macmillan, London, 2020, p. 1.
107. Ibid., p. 6.
108. Ibid., pp. 11, 12.
109. A. Carter, 'Puss-in-Boots', in Tesdell (ed.), *Cat Stories*, pp. 357, 358, 360.
110. Ibid., pp. 361–2.
111. Ibid., p. 377.
112. Saki, 'Tobermory', in Brown (ed.), *Classic Cat Stories*, p. 313.
113. Ibid., p. 315.
114. Ibid., p. 316
115. S.V. Benét, 'The King of the Cats', in Brown (ed.), *Classic Cat Stories*, p. 209.
116. Ibid., p. 220.
117. P. Highsmith, 'Ming's Biggest Prey', in Tesdell (ed.), *Cat Stories*, p. 191.
118. N. Soseki, *I Am a Cat*, Tuttle, North Clarendon VT, 2002, p. 1.
119. M.J. Engh, 'The Tail', in Bill Fawcett (ed.), *Cats in Space and Other Places*, Simon & Schuster, New York, 1992, p. 173.
120. E. Hemingway, *In Our Time*, Charles Scribner's Sons, New York, 1958, p. 121.
121. A. Nastasi, *Writers and Their Cats*, Chronicle, San Francisco, 2018, p. 24.
122. W.S. Burroughs, *The Cat Inside*, Penguin, London, 1992, p. 17.
123. J. Kerouac, *Big Sur*, Penguin Classics, London, 2012, p. 45.
124. E.A. Poe, *The Works of Edgar Allan Poe*, vol. I, Collier & Son, New York, 1903, Preface; www.gutenberg.org/files/2147/2147-h/2147-h.htm.
125. M. Weiss, 'Poe's Catterina', *Mississippi Quarterly*, vol. 19, no. 1, 1965–66, p. 30.
126. J.C. Oates, 'Jubilate: An Homage in Catterel* Verse', *New Yorker*, 28 July 2015.
127. V.S. Naipaul, 'The Strangeness of Grief', *New Yorker*, 30 December 2019.
128. B. Hrabal, *All My Cats*, Penguin Classics, London, 2019, p. 43.
129. N. Gaiman, 'The Price', in Tesdell (ed.), *Cat Stories*, p. 226.
130. Nastasi, *Writers and Their Cats*, p. 24.
131. A.C. Clarke, 'Who's There?', in Fawcett (ed.), *Cats in Space and Other Places*, p. 102.
132. J.R. Conly, 'Tales of a Starship's Cat', in Fawcett (ed.), *Cats in Space and Other Places*, p. 95.
133. A.E. van Vogt, 'Black Destroyer', in Fawcett (ed.), *Cats in Space and Other Places*, p. 279.
134. D. Ketterer, *Canadian Science Fiction and Fantasy*, Indiana University Press, Bloomington IN, 1992, pp. 45–7.
135. F. Brown, 'Mouse', in Fawcett (ed.), *Cats in Space and Other Places*, p. 26.
136. M. Haushofer, *The Wall*, trans. S. Whiteside, Quartet, London, 2013, p. 13.
137. Ibid., p. 40.

138. T. Gautier, *My Private Menagerie*, in *The Works of Theophile Gautier*, vol. 19, John Wilson, Cambridge, 1902; www.gutenberg.org/files/30760/30760-h/30760-h.htm.

139. M. Joseph, *Cat's Company*, Michael Joseph, London, 1946, p. 32.

140. M. Joseph, *Charles: The Story of a Friendship*, Michael Joseph, London, 1943, p. 6.

141. Ibid., p. 47.

142. D. O'Connor, *Paw Tracks in the Moonlight*, Constable, London, 2009, p. 89.

143. G. Cooper, *Homer's Odyssey*, Bantam, London, 2010, p. 43.

144. esol.britishcouncil.org/content/learners/skills/reading/british-worst-learning-languages.

145. J. Hankins, 'Stroke of Good Fortune', *Guardian*, 2 March 2002.

146. T. Hiraide, *The Guest Cat*, trans. E. Selland, Picador, London, 2014, p. 29.

147. Ibid., p. 11.

148. Ibid., p. 69.

149. I. Boyashov, *The Way of Muri*, trans. A.L. Darragh, Hesperus, London, 2012, p. 22.

FURTHER READING

Aberconway, C. (ed.), *Dictionary of Cat Lovers*, Michael Joseph, London, 1949.

Aesop, *Aesop's Fables*, trans. V.S. Vernon Jones, Avenel Books, New York, 1912.

Aesop, *The Aesop for Children*, illus. M. Winter, Rand McNally, Chicago, 1912.

Aesop, 2011, *Aesop's Fables*, Project Gutenberg, www.gutenberg.org/cache/epub/28/pg28.html.

Alcott, L.M., *Little Women*, Xist Classics, Tustin CA, 2014.

Aldiss, B.W., *The Cat Improvement Co.*, Green Cat Press, Salt Lake City UT, 2004.

Apollinaire, G., 'The Cat', https://thefirelizard.wordpress.com/tag/guillaume-apollinaire.

Arikawa, H., *The Travelling Cat Chronicles*, Doubleday, London, 2017.

Arslanian, T., and A. Marttila, *Shop Cats of New York*, Harper, New York, 2016.

Atwood, M., 'Mourning for Cats', in *The Door*, Virago, London, 2009.

Baillie, J., 'The Kitten', www.poetrynook.com/poem/kitten-0.

Baxter, C., *The Sun Collective*, Pantheon, New York, 2020.

Benét, S.V., 'The King of the Cats', in Becky Brown (ed.), *Classic Cat Stories*, Macmillan, London, 2020.

Bowen, J., *A Street Cat Named Bob*, Hodder & Stoughton, London, 2012.

Boyashov, I., *The Way of Muri*, trans. A.L. Darragh, Hesperus, London, 2012.

Brontë, A., *Agnes Grey*, Thomas Cautley Newby, London, 1847.

Brown, B. (ed.), *Classic Cat Stories*, Macmillan, London, 2020.

Brown, F., 'Mouse', in Bill Fawcett (ed.), *Cats in Space and Other Places*, Simon & Schuster, New York, 1992.

Bulgakov, M., *The Master and Margarita*, Vintage, London, 2004.

Bunson, M., *The Vampire Encyclopedia*, Gramercy Books, New York, 1993.

Burroughs, W.S., *The Cat Inside*, Penguin Classics, London, 1992.

Butcher, J., *The Aeronaut's Windlass*, Orbit, London, 2015.

Capote, T., *Breakfast at Tiffany's*, Penguin Classics, London, 2000.

Carroll, L., *Alice's Adventures in Wonderland*, illus. J. Tenniel, Maynard, Merrill, New York, 1895.

Carter, A., 'Puss-in-Boots', in Diana Secker Tesdell (ed.), *Cat Stories*, Everyman, New York, 2011.

Cheyrrh, C.J., *The Chanur Saga*, Penguin Putnum, New York, 2000.

Clampitt, C., *Critical Survey of Mythology & Folklore: Gods & Goddesses*, Salem Press, Amenia NY, 2019.

Clarke, A.C., 'Who's There?', in Bill Fawcett (ed.), *Cats in Space and Other Places*, Simon & Schuster, New York, 1992.

Colette, *Gigi* and *The Cat*, trans. R. Senhouse and A. White, Vintage, London, 2001.

Collins, S., *Catching Fire*, Scholastic, London, 2013.

Collins, S., *The Hunger Games*, Scholastic, London, 2013.

Collins, S., *Mockingjay*, Scholastic, London, 2013.

Conly, J.R., 'Tales of a Starship's Cat', in Bill Fawcett (ed.), *Cats in Space and Other Places*, Simon & Schuster, New York, 1992.

Cooper, G., *Homer's Odyssey*, Bantam, London, 2010.

Cowper, W., 'The Retired Cat', www.luminarium.org/eightlit/cowper/cat.htm.

Davies, W.H., 'The Cat', www.poetryexplorer.net/poem.php?id=10024954.

Defoe, D., *The Life and Adventures of Robinson Crusoe*, Harper, London, 2010.

De Vries, C., *I and Claudius: Travels With My Cat*, Bloomsbury, London, 1999.

Dickens, C., *Bleak House*, Hurd & Houghton, New York, 1869.

Dickens, C., *The Uncommercial Traveller*, Chapman & Hall, London, 1905.

Dickens, C., *The Personal History of David Copperfield*, University Society Publishers, New York, 1908.

Dickens, C., *The Life and Adventures of Nicholas Nickleby*, Macmillan, London, 1916.

Dickens, C., *Great Expectations*, Alma Books, London, 2014.

Diesel, A., 'Felines and Female Divinities: The Association of Cats with Goddesses, Ancient and Contemporary', *Journal for the Study of Religion*, vol. 21, no. 1, 2008, pp. 71–94.

Divani, L., *Seven Lives and One Great Love: Memoirs of a Cat*, trans. K. Matsoukas, Europa Editions, New York, 2014.

Dodd, L., *Slinky Malinki: Catflaps*, Puffin Books, London, 2000.

Donaldson, J., *Tabby McTat*, illus. A. Scheffler, Alison Green Books, London, 2009.

Dostoevsky, F., *Crime and Punishment*, Lerner, Minneapolis MN, 2015.

Dr. Seuss, *The Cat in the Hat*, HarperCollins, London, 2017.

Edgerton, F., *The Panchatantra Reconstructed*, American Oriental Society, New Haven CT, 1924.

Eliot, T.S., *Old Possum's Book of Practical Cats*, Faber & Faber, London, 2015.

Ende, M., *The Night of Wishes*, trans. H. Schwarzbauer and R. Takvorian, illus. R. Kehn, New York Review Children's Collection, New York, 2017.

Engels, D., *Classical Cats*, Routledge, Abingdon, 2001.

Engh, M.J., 'The Tail', in Bill Fawcett (ed.), *Cats in Space and Other Places*, Simon & Schuster, New York, 1992.

Fitzgerald, F.S., *The Great Gatsby*, Penguin, London, 2000.

Frost, G., *Lyrec*, Ace Original Fantasy, New York, 1984.

Gaiman, N., 'The Price', in Diana Secker Tesdell (ed.), *Cat Stories*, Everyman, New York, 2011.

Gaiman, N., *Coraline*, Bloomsbury, London, 2013.

Gardener, S., *Three Pickled Herrings*, illus. D. Roberts, Orion, London, 2013.

Gautier, T., *My Private Menagerie*, in *The Works of Theophile Gautier*, vol. 19, John Wilson and Son, Cambridge, 1902.

Gayton, S., *His Royal Whiskers*, illus. P. Cottrill, Andersen Press, London, 2017.

Goethe, J.W., *Reynard the Fox*, John C. Nimmo, London, 1887.

Gravett, E., *Matilda's Cat*, Macmillan, London, 2012.

Gray, K., *Oi, Cat!*, illus. J. Field, Hodder, London, 2017.

Gray, T., 'Ode on the Death of a Favourite Cat Drowned in a Tub of Goldfishes', www.poetryfoundation.org/poems/44302/ode-on-the-death-of-a-favourite-cat-drowned-in-a-tub-of-goldfishes.

Hale, K., *Orlando the Marmalade Cat: A Camping Holiday*, Puffin, London, 2014.

Hankins, J., 'Stroke of good fortune', *Guardian*, 2 March 2002.

Hardy, T., *Tess of the d'Urbervilles*, Macmillan, London, 1912; www.gutenberg.org/files/110/110-h/110-h.htm.

Hardy, T., 'Last Words to a Dumb Friend', www.poemhunter.com/poem/last-words-to-a-dumb-friend.

Haushofer, M., *The Wall*, trans. S. Whiteside, Quartet, London, 2013.

Heine, H., 'Songs of Creation', in *The Poems of Heine*, George Bell, London, 1908; www.gutenberg.org/files/52882/52882-h/52882-h.htm.

Heinlein, R.A., *The Cat Who Walks through Walls*, New English Library, London, 1985.

Heinlein, R.A., *To Sail Beyond the Sunset*, Ace, New York, 1987.

Heinlein, R.A., 'Ordeal in Space', in Bill Fawcett (ed.), *Cats in Space and Other Places*, Simon & Schuster, New York, 1992.

Hemingway, E., *In Our Time*, Charles Scribner's Sons, New York, 1958.

Herrick, R., 'A Country Life', www.luminarium.org/sevenlit/herrick/thomas.htm.

Herrick, R., 'His Grange, or Private Wealth', www.luminarium.org/sevenlit/herrick/grange.htm.

Highsmith, P., 'Ming's Biggest Prey', in Diana Secker Tesdell (ed.), *Cat Stories*, Everyman's Library, New York, 2011.

Hiraide, T., *The Guest Cat*, trans. E. Selland, Picador, London, 2014.

Hoffman, E.T.A., *The Life and Opinions of the Tomcat Murr together with a Fragmentary Biography of Kapellmeister Johannes Kreisler on Random Sheets of Waste Paper*, Penguin Classics, London, 1999.

Hrabal, B., *All My Cats*, Penguin Classics, London, 2019.

Hunter, E., *Warrior Cats: Into the Wild*, HarperCollins, London, 2003.

Jackson, S., *We Have Always Lived in the Castle*, Penguin, London, 2009.

Joseph, M., *Charles: The Story of a Friendship*, Michael Joseph, London, 1943.

Joseph, M., *Cat's Company*, Michael Joseph, London, 1946.

Joyce, J., *Ulysses*, Booklassic, Csorna, 2015.

Kashdan, J.G., 'Reynard the Fox', in *Masterplots*, 4th edn, Salem Press, Amenia NY, 2010.

Kawamura, G., *If Cats Disappeared From The World*, trans. E. Selland, Picador, London, 2018.

Kerouac, J., *Big Sur*, Penguin Classics, London, 2012.

Kerr, J., *Mog the Forgetful Cat*, William Collins, London, 1970.

Kerr, J., *Creatures*, HarperCollins, London, 2013.

Kerr, J., *Katinka's Tail*, HarperCollins, London, 2018.

Ketterer, D., *Canadian Science Fiction and Fantasy*, Indiana University Press, Bloomington IN, 1992.

King, S., *Pet Sematary*, Hodder & Stoughton, London, 1989.

Kipling, R., 'The Cat That Walked by Himself', in Becky Brown (ed.), *Classic Cat Stories*, Macmillan, London, 2020.

Kitamura, S., 'Me and My Cat', www.youtube.com/watch?v=eDzISc6o_Xs.

Lane, E.W. (trans.), *The Thousand and One Nights*, Chatto & Windus, London, 1912.

Lane, V., and T. White, *London Pubcats*, Paradise Road, Dagenham, 2016.

Lawrence, D.H., *Women in Love*, Cambridge University Press, Cambridge, 1987.

Lawrence, D.H., *Lady Chatterley's Lover*, Arcadia, London, 2013.

Le Guin, U., 'Schrödinger's Cat', in Bill Fawcett (ed.), *Cats in Space and Other Places*, Simon & Schuster, New York, 1992.

Leiber, F., 'Space-Time for Springers', in Diana Secker Tesdell (ed.), *Cat Stories*, Everyman, New York, 2011.

Lessing, D., 'Jellicles, Gumbies and Others', *Spectator*, vol. 290, no. 9093, November 2002.

Lessing, D., 'An Old Woman and Her Cat', in Diana Secker Tesdell (ed.), *Cat Stories*, Everyman, New York, 2011.

Lloyd, S., *Mr Pusskins. Best in Show*, Orchard Books, London, 2008.

The Mahābhārata, trans. Kisari Mohan Ganguli, 1883–96, www.gutenberg. org/cache/epub/15476/pg15476.html.

Mann, J., *From Aesop to Reynard: Beast Literature in Medieval Britain*, Oxford University Press, Oxford, 2009.

McCaffrey, A., and E. Scarborough, *Catalyst: A Tale of the Barque Cats*, Del Rey, London, 2010.

Moore, K., *Felix the Railway Cat*, Penguin, London, 2017.

Morpurgo, M., *Kaspar, Prince of Cats*, HarperCollins, London, 2010.

Munro, H., 'Milk for the Cat', www.poemhunter.com/poem/ milk-for-the-cat.

Murakami, H., *The Wind-Up Bird Chronicle*, Knopf, New York, 1997.

Murakami, H., *Kafka on the Shore*, Harvill, London, 2005.

Murphy, J., *The Worst Witch*, Puffin Books, London, 2013.

Myron, V., *Dewey: The Small-town Library-cat Who Touched the World*, Hodder & Stoughton, London, 2009.

Naipaul, V.S., 'The Strangeness of Grief', *New Yorker*, 30 December 2019.

Nastasi, A., *Writers and Their Cats*, Chronicle, San Francisco, 2018.

Nicoll, H., *Meg on the Moon*, illus. J. Pieńkowski, Puffin, London, 1973.

Nikolajeva, M., 'Devils, Demons, Familiars, Friends: Towards a Semiotics of Literary Cats', *Marvels & Tales*, vol. 23, no. 2, 2009, pp. 248–66.

Niven, L., et al., *The Man-Kzin Wars*, Baen, New York, 2013.

Nizamoglu, C., 2007, 'Cats in Islamic Culture', *Muslim Heritage*, https:// muslimheritage.com/cats-islamic-culture/#ftn111.

Nordqvist, S., *When Findus Was Little and Disappeared*, Hawthorn Press, Stroud, 2008.

Nye, J.L., 'Well Worth the Money', in Bill Fawcett (ed.), *Cats in Space and Other Places*, Simon & Schuster, New York, 1992.

Oates, J.C., 'Jubilate: An Homage in Catterel* Verse', *New Yorker*, 28 July 2015.

O'Connor, D., *Paw Tracks in the Moonlight*, Constable, London, 2009.

Opler, M.E., 'Japanese Folk Belief Concerning the Cat', *Journal of the Washington Academy of Sciences*, vol. 35, no. 9, 1945, pp. 269–75.

Orwell, G., *Animal Farm*, Mariner, Boston MA, 1989.

'Pangur Bán', http://irisharchaeology.ie/2013/10/pangur-ban.

Perrault, C., 'Puss in Boots', in Becky Brown (ed.), *Classic Cat Stories*, Macmillan, London, 2020.

Piggott, J., *Japanese Mythology*, Paul Hamlyn, London, 1969.

Poe, E.A., 'The Black Cat', in Diana Secker Tesdell (ed.), *Cat Stories*, Everyman, New York, 2011.

Potter, B., *The Story of Miss Moppet*, F. Warne, New York, 1906.

Potter, B., *The Tale of Tom Kitten*, F. Warne, New York, 1907.

Potter, B., *The Roly-Poly Pudding*, F. Warne, New York, 1908.

Pratchett, T., *The Unadulterated Cat*, Orion, London, 2002.

Pratchett, T., *The Amazing Maurice and his Educated Rodents*, Corgi, London, 2004.

Pratchett, T., *Witches Abroad*, Transworld, London, 2010.

Pratchett, T., *Wyrd Sisters*, Transworld, London, 2010.

Pullman, P., *The Amber Spyglass*, Scholastic, London, 2007.

Pullman, P., *Northern Lights*, Scholastic, London, 2007.

Pullman, P., *The Subtle Knife*, Scholastic, London, 2007.

Riddell, C., *Ottoline and the Yellow Cat*, Macmillan, London, 2010.

Rogers, K.M., *Cat*, Reaktion Books, London, 2019.

Rowling, J.K., *Harry Potter and the Prisoner of Azkaban*, Bloomsbury, London, 2017.

Roy, N., *The Wildings*, Pushkin Press, London, 2016.

Said, S.F., *Varjak Paw*, illus. D. McKean, Corgi, London, 2014

Saki, 'Tobermory', in Becky Brown (ed.), *Classic Cat Stories*, Macmillan, London, 2020.

Sharratt, N., *The Cat and the King*, Alison Green Books, London, 2016.

Serpell, J.A., 'Domestication and History of the Cat', in Dennis C. Turner and Patrick Bateson (eds), *The Domestic Cat*, Cambridge University Press, Cambridge, 2013, pp. 83–100.

Sleigh, B., *Carbonel*, Puffin Books, London, 2015.

Smart, C., 'My Cat Jeoffry', www.poetryfoundation.org/poems/45173/jubilate-agno.

Smith, C., 'The Game of Rat and Dragon' and 'The Ballad of Lost C'Mell', in Bill Fawcett (ed.), *Cats in Space and Other Places*, Simon & Schuster, New York, 1992.

Sorosiak, C., *My Life as a Cat*, Nosy Crow, London, 2020.

Soseki, N., *I Am a Cat*, Tuttle, North Clarendon VT, 2002.

Statovci, P., *My Cat Yugoslavia*, trans. D. Hackston, Pushkin Press, London, 2017.

Stoker, B., *Dracula*, Penguin Books, London, 2003.

Surman, R., *Cathedral Cats*, Collins, London, 2005.

Swift, J., *Gulliver's Travels*, Lerner Publishing Group, Minneapolis MN, 2015.

Tanizaki, J., *A Cat, A Man, and Two Women*, Daunt, London, 2017.

Tesdell, D. Secker (ed.), *Cat Stories*, Everyman, New York, 2011.

Twain, M. *The Adventures of Tom Sawyer*, Samizdat Press, Orange CT.

Twain, M., 'Dick Baker's Cat', in Becky Brown (ed.), *Classic Cat Stories*, Macmillan Collector's Library, London, 2020.

Van Vogt, A.E., 'Black Destroyer', in Bill Fawcett (ed.), *Cats in Space and Other Places*, Simon & Schuster, New York, 1992.

Voake, C., *Ginger Finds a Home*, Walker Books, London, 2008.

Vocelle, L.A., *Revered and Reviled: A Complete History of the Domestic Cat*, Great Cat Publications, 2017.

Weiss, M., 'Poe's Catterina', *Mississippi Quarterly*, vol. 19, no. 1, 1965–66, pp. 29–33.

W.H.N., 'Edgar Allan Poe: An Appreciation', in *Works of Edgar Allan Poe*, vol. 1, Collier & Son, New York, 1903; www.gutenberg.org/files/2147/2147-h/2147-h.htm.

Williams, T., *Tailchaser's Song*, Hodder & Stoughton, London, 2015.

Willy, C., *Barks and Purrs*, trans. M. Kelly, Desmond Fitzgerald, New York, 1913.

Woolf, V., *Between the Acts*, Vintage, London, 1992.

Woolf, V., *A Room of One's Own*, Oxford University Press, Oxford, 2015.

Zola, É., *Nana*, Penguin Classics, London, 1972.

Zola, É., *Thérèse Raquin*, Vintage, London, 2014.

INDEX